THE HAMMERFIELD GAMBIT

THE SCIENCE OFFICER: VOLUME 7

BLAZE WARD

KNOTTED ROAD PRESS

The Hammerfield Gambit
Volume 7
Blaze Ward
Copyright © 2017 Blaze Ward
All rights reserved
Published by Knotted Road Press
www.KnottedRoadPress.com

ISBN: 978-1-943663-60-6

Never miss a release!
If you'd like to be notified of new releases, sign up for my newsletter.

I only send out newsletters once a quarter, will never spam you, or use your email for nefarious purposes. You can also unsubscribe at any time.

http://www.blazeward.com/newsletter/

Other Science Fiction Stories

Myrmirdons

Moonshot

Menelaus

Earthquake Gun

Moscow Gold

Fairchild

White Crane

The Collective **Universe**

The Shipwrecked Mermaid

Imposters

BOOK TWENTY-ONE:
VISITORS

PART ONE

It had been a year this morning.

Behnam let her thoughts wander without any particular order as she meditated in a full lotus, letting the artificial sun warm her golden-brown nudity. A light breeze, warm and languid, came out of the area designated east and blew across the vast, blue lake that filled the center of her tremendous starship.

It was not the biggest vessel in the sector. That title was held by a class of monstrous freighters that hauled millions of shipping containers at a time, plying routes between major worlds and capitals.

But *Shangdu* was absolutely the most luxurious. The most prestigious.

The most coveted.

As she sat on a towel on her glorious, white-sand beach, next to her private, indoor lake, on her personal starship resort, the *Khatum of Altai* contemplated security, both her own, and that of her guests.

It was among the best in the galaxy, that security. Certainly, a fantastically expensive overhead, but necessary.

Altai was a moderately wealthy planet, as they went. 1.4

billion inhabitants. Generally well-educated. A largely meritocratic society which valued inherited wealth far less than personal success, enforced with ruthlessly-tight laws on inheritance.

You did not get to take it with you. You also did not get to leave it to your heirs. So it was worth it to citizens to fund the arts and education as their legacy.

With exactly one exception.

The *Khatum of Altai* owned the planet. *In fee simple.* She maintained a government back home as she traveled, and personally oversaw the installation of each Prime Minister, and approved every flag officer promoted to a position from which they might be a danger to her and her power.

At the same time, she wasn't all that onerous as an overlord.

People liked to think of her personal megayacht, the super-luxury resort *Shangdu*, as a playground for the wealthy elite, the most driven men and women, where your personal success was your invitation, not your family wealth.

It was a system that had worked for thirty years now since a group of misguided, disgruntled military officers had assassinated her parents and siblings. They'd thought they could control the throne in the body of the youngest daughter away at school.

They had not expected the woman that had returned. The avenging angel. It had been a lethal surprise, at least on their part.

For thirty years, security had been her focus.

Pleasure, as well, if only secondarily. With that level of wealth, she could build and maintain a personal yacht that was among the fifty largest vessels in space, staffed with thousands and flying from point to point while entertaining people who could afford her astronomical rates and pass her background checks.

At the same time, education factored high in her life. Both keeping her own mind sharp, and seeing to the instruction of her four children, now all older than she had been when she came to the throne.

Soon, she would need to address inheritance.

One would become the heir. Three would be married off and sent their own way, no longer a threat to Behnam or whichever sibling came to prominence.

Security.

Only once had her systems and planning ever truly failed her, minor swindles and white lies notwithstanding.

And even that one had been a pleasant failure: a hard pirate of a man, but one marked by honor and intellect, plus the stamina to keep up with her.

Just passing through, as he had said. A thief in the night, no threat to her personally, only to one of her guests, and even then only a philosophical threat, and not physical.

And then he had gone.

Behnam ran her hands through the warm sand around her beach towel, let the breeze swirl it back into the sedge grass in the small bowl behind her.

She had first laid eyes on the man in this very spot.

Had it been an entire year ago?

It had. The day was burned into her memory, not for what he did, but for what he hadn't done.

All that power at his fingertips, and he had still been a man cutting a diamond, rather than an arsonist destroying a forest.

A year ago today. Here. And then gone.

Behnam contained a sigh.

Likely, the man would never return. He had that air about him.

Hard. Driven. Smart.

Capable.

But also emotionally sound and empathic.

So unlike most of the men and women at that level of success. At least the ones who passed through *Shangdu*. The vast majority of them tended towards amoral psychopaths or scoundrels.

She missed him.

Footsteps approached on the sand before their owner came into sight.

She had chosen this spot for the memory. Captain Navarre had chosen it for its relative isolation.

The crunch suggested boots, rather than bare feet. The sound of wheezing came close behind, so someone not in shape to tromp across sand dunes on an artificial beach, two hundred light years from home.

She recognized the wheezing. Perhaps it was time to make the man give up all the rich foods and spend more time exercising. She had valued him as a bureaucrat too much to nag, but his health was suffering. And she would need his canny intellect and bloodthirstiness soon.

Tömörbaatar's head appeared first, capped with the little box cap in white silk that he had first effected as a uniform forty years ago and kept ever since.

Behnam could remember first meeting the man, when he had served her father. A few people had laughed out loud at his fashion sense then. None of those people were still around.

His name meant *Iron Hero*. If he was a squishy, middle-aged man with a wispy beard gone gray, Tömörbaatar was still a deadly player in the political arena. Her throne was safe, with men like him serving her.

Him being here now, however, was not a good sign. Anything less critical could have waited until their regular briefing this afternoon.

Behnam unfolded her long legs and rose in a single motion, grasping the towel that had been beneath her and wrapping it around her hips.

It was not modesty. Tömörbaatar had seen her nude before.

Him coming to her meant she was needed elsewhere. Now. And she might not have listened to anyone else's request.

This must be big.

She did not need to worry about towering over the man, with her five extra centimeters of height, even while he wore boots with heels.

Nothing in the universe had ever been found to intimidate the *Iron Hero of Altai*.

"What is it?" Behnam asked simply as he got close enough to speak politely.

It was a measure of his place with her that Tömörbaatar could stop and bend forward enough to gasp for a few beats before he spoke. Anyone else would find such disrespectful behavior grounds for termination and eviction.

"A warship has arrived in system, Your Grace," he said finally, still wheezing but improving as his heart rate fell. He must have literally run here with the news.

"Whose?" she asked sharply.

They were currently in orbit of *Binhai*, a planet with loose affiliations with the largest and most dangerous of the interstellar nations today, *The Concord*.

Tömörbaatar got a dangerous gleam in his eyes.

"They are flying no flag, Your Grace," he said simply.

"You said warship, Iron Hero," she replied. "The only other option would be pirates, would it not?"

"Indeed," he agreed. "All gun crews are on station, waiting."

"You think a frigate flying a black flag is a threat?" she asked.

"This is no frigate, Your Grace," he countered. "According to the encyclopedia, it is a *First Rate Galleon* of a type manufactured by *Neu Berne*, in the previous century. It would be comparable to a *Concord* cruiser for firepower. They might be able to destroy us, if they chose, but not without suffering grievous damage in the process."

"What do they want?" she asked, feeling the blood drain out of her face.

In thirty years, she had never been in a situation like this. *Shangdu* was a recreational warship, where the safety of very wealthy passengers was assured. Armed and capable, but a resort, not a military installation.

It would require significant risk to challenge that.

"The young woman demanded to speak with you, personally," her primary assistant, her right hand, responded. "Nobody else."

The warm air was suddenly not warm enough. Or the chill that was pervading her was psychological, and not physical.

Goosebumps rose on her skin.

What would a pirate warship want with her?

PART TWO

Free.

After years locked inside those two, tiny survey probes, Suvi luxuriated in the solar wind flowing across her skin again, like a phoenix kissed by the flames.

Better, she was back in a warship.

The *Concord* vessel that would come to be known as *Mielikki* had been downgraded to a mere probe-cutter when she was demobilized, after the end of the Great War and all the subsequent silliness. One hundred and five years as a *Concord* Yeoman, then four good years with Javier before the pirates had killed her.

And now, she was back. Bigger than she had been before by three point four orders of magnitude.

Badder, too.

The *Sentience-in-residence* on what had been the *Neu Berne* First Rate Galleon, *Hammerfield*, last flagship of the *Neu Berne* fleet before those people had lost the Great War.

Hell on wheels.

Suvi reached out with the sensors that had been her eyes once, aboard *Mielikki*, before the pirate strike corvette *Storm Gauntlet* had taken them. The eyes of a probe-cutter.

Better than an eagle.

The vacuum of space didn't have a smell, but it did tickle. And it was filled with radio chatter, encrypted and clear, on every channel and frequency she chose to listen to, all the way down to the gurgling hiss of *Binhai's* star as it transformed hydrogen into light, heat, and age.

Suvi ignored most of the noise. She was really only interested in one vessel, among the hundreds in front of her orbiting *Binhai,* as well as the ones coming or going.

Shangdu.

The personal pleasure yacht of one of the wealthiest people in space, the *Khatum of Altai.*

They had never been formally introduced. Javier had been busy pretending to be Captain Navarre, and Suvi had been pretending to be about as smart as a rabbit, hiding in the tiny survey probe.

And Behnam Sherazi had been pretending to be either a cold, aloof aristocrat, or a bored dilettante seeking mindless pleasure.

That game probably worked on anybody that couldn't scan your respiration, heart rate, and pupil dilation from across the room to put lie to the careful stories you have cocooned yourself in.

Not that Suvi would do anything with the information.

Javier might actually be smitten, this time.

Suvi had made a study of the physiological changes that came over the man when the topic of the *Khatum* came up. He liked women, and maintained polite, intimate, physical relationships with many members of the crew.

None of them affected him like just thinking about *that woman* did.

Suvi suppressed a jealous rage that she couldn't have a physical body, just so she could compete. She really didn't need anyone explaining CG Jung's theories to her, since she could read the original texts herself.

She had Javier's mind, and his love. That would be enough.

Hopefully.

Because as a First Rate Galleon, she was likely to outlive the man by centuries, if she was careful. What would her distant future bring?

A signal brought all her little avatars, her *shards of consciousness*, back together. More or less.

Shangdu was responding, the big, armed yacht slowly orbiting *Binhai*'s skies while Suvi sat in her armored warhorse clear out at the edge of polite communication range.

Five light-seconds lag would annoy the hell out of an organic. At seventeen thousand times human processing speed, she had time to spare, so Suvi sat herself down in her favorite chair, turned her desk into a three-deck grand piano, and started composing music.

For fun, and because the limits to being an AI revolved around how silly a girl could dream, Suvi added two more arms to herself and started pounding the keys with all four hands at once.

Seventeen bars in, she smiled and started over, spinning up a couple of rock improvisation sub-routines: a drummer and a standing bass player, then let them riff on her as she went.

No jazz today. Or rather, a hard, symphonic jazz that was more than just individual expertise with an instrument but instead walked right over into emotional story-telling.

Not that she would probably ever let anyone alive today hear this particular tune. Jung would have had a field-day with her.

Finally, the full signal arrived. Humans, talking at human speed, as it resolved into a face. The woman they had come to see.

Her.

About the only thing the two of them had in common was height. Suvi projected herself at a relative height of 175 cm. Tall for most women. Average for a *Concord* officer, as they tended to be physically impressive creatures.

Behnam Sherazi, the *Khatum of Altai*, stood at 177 cm. She was lush and curvy, while Suvi's body image derived from that of a volleyball player: a tall, lean, hard athlete.

The other woman was dusky as well. The black hair, brown

eyes, and golden-brown skin of what ethnographers would classify as the Central Asian highlands, back on Earth, while Suvi had been originally programmed by Finns from the far northwest of the Eurasian landmass.

Blond, fair, blue-eyed, and slender.

Everything this other woman was not.

And electronic, to boot.

"I am the *Khatum of Altai*," the woman announced in a firm voice, tinged with an underlying thread of annoyance at having been *summoned*.

Nothing more. Just those words.

Suvi reverted her primary communications avatar to baseline to compose a reply.

Four-armed weirdoes would only make the situation even stranger than it was about to get.

Not that she was worried. *Hammerfield* had inherited the two Pulse Cannon turrets and the Ion Pulsar off of *Storm Gauntlet* to replace three of her older, existing weapon systems. Between that and her already existent suite, Suvi could do a tremendous amount of damage to any vessel short of a *Concord Warmaster*.

Still, they were here to be polite.

Hopefully.

She opened a channel and sent a message pulse back.

"This is the private-service, cargo vessel *Excalibur*," she transmitted under a simple encryption key. Just enough to keep amateurs at bay. "Requesting permission to rendezvous with your vessel and send over a group to discuss a possible business arrangement with you personally."

And *transmit*.

Nothing more. Nothing incriminating.

Yet.

Back to the keyboard.

Something martial this time, so she added a full horn section and told them to raise the rafters, plus a pair of dueling electric guitars to underline the keyboards. She would have at least twenty seconds, maybe thirty, before she got a reply.

"Who?" came back less than twelve seconds later. The tone was guarded. Verging on a rude reply, but withholding for now.

Twelve seconds? With ten of those seconds spent in transit? No dithering. No thought. Damn.

Suvi suddenly appreciated just how smart, canny, and dangerous Behnam Sherazi was.

"Eutrupio," Suvi sent immediately. "And guests."

If very few people knew that Captain Navarre existed, only a handful were aware that the man even had a first name. Javier had told her that the *Khatum* was one of that handful.

Inside knowledge was an even better way to encrypt things.

"Granted."

Again, twelve seconds round-trip.

Apparently, the *Khatum of Altai* hadn't forgotten Captain Navarre. Hopefully, she hadn't been lying about forgiving him.

Because if anything happened to Javier, Suvi would see that bitch reduced to a cold plasma cloud.

PART THREE

Javier took one last look in the mirror.

His hair was getting long enough he probably should have had it cut, but he was afraid at how much gray would have infiltrated the blackish-brown that had been there for four and a half decades.

Likewise, the chin was shaved smooth, having already largely succumbed to white.

After stealing this ship, the former *Neu Berne* flagship *Hammerfield*, and all the work to make her right again, he had upped his weekly workout routine as well. More running. More stairs. More yoga.

The results hadn't been immediately obvious, because most of his clothes were already designed to be loose and comfy.

It was only when he put on something older that he realized just how much bulk he had lost. Very little weight, but centimeters gone here and added there. He was more Vee-shaped now than he used to be. And he needed a new belt, as his waist kept shrinking.

'Mina, Dr. Wilhelmina Teague, *Shepherd of the Word*, wasn't here, so he could take what he thought of as Navarre's uniform, and toss it into the back of the closet, settling for a look that was more in line with a businessman who occasionally dabbled in freelance piracy.

A tall, bald stevedore named Adrian Ahmad, a crewman with a bent for costuming, had crafted the ensemble. And done so with a deft touch and obvious enthusiasm. He had even lightly propositioned Javier a few times along the way, but had responded well to a gentle no.

It wasn't that Javier wouldn't. He just preferred women. And had a smorgasbord to pick from on this ship.

Maybe later. After he had used the man's fashion cunning to utterly annihilate everyone he was about to meet today.

Because Adrian had managed the look that would impress everyone, hands down.

Maroon silk jacket embroidered in gold on the chest and arms, playing on Navarre's original coloring. Done in a sherwani style: knee-length and tailored to his silhouette with a full row of buttons. Short, standing collar. Buttoned to his waist and then falling slowly open in a flair to mid-thigh. Cut to fit his shoulders and hips in ways that made every woman who looked at him lick her lips unconsciously.

It was nice feeling awesome.

The sash tied around his waist outside the jacket and knotted on his left hip was gold silk as well, and contained a few interesting, hidden pockets for gear. The outfit also included a belt for holding a pistol and a sword, but he had left the rig in the closet today. It would send the wrong message, anyway.

The combat britches had been reborn. No longer padded leather for protection, these were done in silk as well, gold this time, in the same heavy weight as the jacket, but not armored, and instead tucked into those twenty-ring, shiny, black boots with the maroon laces.

Javier had kept those. Just walking decks in that much weight centered his mind into the awful, brutal place that was Captain Eutrupio Navarre, killer-extraordinaire.

He really didn't need it, but other folks would have to be impressed into their place if he was going to pull this off.

"Gorgeous," her voice came from the speaker, agreeing with his assessment.

Suvi wasn't there in the room with him anymore.

Still, Javier had left the two empty probes on a nearby shelf as reminders, since she was the whole vessel around him now, a warm, comforting blanket that took him back to the days when it had just been the two of them, sailing boldly into the unknown.

Javier slept better than he had in years.

He released a deep sigh at this point, down in the privacy of what had been Admiral Erica Steiner's suite, back when this vessel had been in service to *Neu Berne* as their flagship. It was more space than he needed, but Captain Sokolov had insisted on taking over the space once held by Captain Ulrich Mayer, *Hammerfield*'s last commander.

It kind of set a new tone to their relationship as well. Hopefully a better one.

Javier wasn't a slave anymore, and Zakhar Sokolov was no longer his owner, however technical that term had been at the time.

Once this pirate war was over, they would need to have a long talk about the next twenty years. Six months ago, Javier had been staring at this very hull from the outside, waiting for it to kill him.

Before he had learned the truth. And found the perfect tool for his vengeance.

"Thank you," Javier finally replied to Suvi, glancing up at a camera tucked into a corner with a smile.

His princess was back in her castle, and nobody would ever take that away from her.

"Status?" he asked.

"Her shuttle has just docked and is waiting for you," Suvi replied. "Zakhar and Djamila are there, greeting a short, Mongolian man in a cute hat. Afia will be along shortly. Piet and I are talking orchestral composition theory up on the bridge."

Javier nodded.

Having an automated warship, commanded by a *Sentience* that didn't need anyone else to fly it, had been a professional threat to Piet Alferdinck, *Storm Gauntlet's* pilot. He could have chosen to leave and find another flying gig, but he and Suvi had bonded over music, of all things.

And Zakhar was grooming the man to become his First Mate, the crew's Executive Officer, now that Javier was no longer in the running for the job. It would be a nice thing.

"Time to go," he said with finality.

The *Khatum* had invited him to not be a stranger, and not an enemy. Had provided him with a cheesecake photo of herself, covered in nothing but long hair and shadows, wearing the Helm of Athena to obscure all of her face except that tremendous smile, kneeling on the bed where they had once romped.

Javier took it as a positive sign as he opened the hatch and set out for the landing bay, well aft and down several decks.

Hopefully, the *Khatum* wasn't about to kill him.

PART FOUR

Javier followed the short, Mongolian guy through hallways he recognized, into places he did not. Zakhar, Djamila, and Afia Burakgazi followed him, the group of them escorted by a pair of extremely quiet men in dark gray uniforms.

Guards. Gendarme.

Bouncers.

Plus Tömörbaatar, possibly more dangerous than any of the muscle boys. Javier could tell that just from the hard look in the man's eyes.

The path had taken them from *Shangdu*'s primary landing bay through the sort of reception area visiting royalty might find impressive. From there, the main corridor through the Elite Class suites, carpeted in moss green with soft blue walls and perfect lighting, until they passed through a semi-hidden doorway into what suddenly looked like Class-A office space.

The carpet here was brown-ish and speckled in that way that would generally hide stains. It was rugged enough to go years without replacing, while the nicer stuff on the outside was probably new annually.

The walls were golden oak boards, about two hands wide and running vertical. Javier assumed they were a veneer over the usual metal bulkheads. The lights were somehow more professional, less warm and inviting than the other ones had been.

Luxury transformed into corporate.

Javier had always expected that this was more like what the woman was, but had never been in a position to ask. Even now, he wasn't sure whether she would throw him out, have him arrested, or make a pass at him.

Or which outcome scared him more.

Best to not waste energy worrying. He was committed at this point, a hog in the chute.

At least he looked better than everyone else. Adrian had guaranteed that. Not that it took much effort, considering how everyone else was dressed today.

Captain Zakhar Sokolov was wearing his personal variant of the standard *Concord* dress uniform, minus all the badges and the tie, but keeping those damned polished-leather black shoes. Olive-green slacks. Lighter green, button-up shirt with a folded collar. Olive-green jacket, single-breasted, with three buttons to his sternum and four stripes on each cuff.

Djamila Sykora, *Dragoon*, was wearing a similar cut of fabric, but in gun-metal gray with blue edging. At 2.1 meters tall, she was a gray tree. At least she wasn't armed today. At least, not carrying any weapons.

The woman *was* a weapon.

Only Afia had treated this like a holiday, and not a possible hanging.

She was wearing what Javier could only describe as harem pants. Diaphanous gold material, mostly translucent, that only gathered at the waist and ankles, over baby blue leggings. A cream-white tunic embroidered with gold dragons that had red eyes and showed off her lean petiteness and golden-brown skin that wasn't much darker than the Khatum's, but more brown and less gold than the other woman.

Both top and bottom seemed to be made with glitter in the fabric, so the smiling engineer was leaving a small cloud of glitter particles everywhere as she walked, slowly infecting the ship with glitter.

Because glitter was forever.

They arrived.

Big, imposing wooden door in dark tones that just screamed *Boardroom*.

Javier sucked a breath deep into his toes and prepared for battle.

Another day. Another drachma.

The short Mongolian dude, Tömörbaatar, knocked briefly, opened the door, and entered, walking around to stand on her right.

The *Khatum of Altai*.

She was even more beautiful than he remembered.

The smile was warm and broad. Welcoming. The eyes, a mischievous twinkle.

Javier didn't know if he should be relieved or worried.

He settled for following Tömörbaatar into the room, coming to rest at the far end of the oval-shaped conference table that dominated the space, a sea of polished wood between them.

There were a handful of her people already seated at that end of the table, but most of them were just bureaucrats handy for taking notes or running errands.

She would make all decisions. He knew that.

Zakhar and Djamila ended up on Javier's right, going forward around the table. Afia took the open chair at his left.

Behnam Sherazi rose from her chair.

Javier didn't care that his eyes couldn't make it back to her face. Even in a charcoal business suit not all that removed from what Sokolov was wearing, she was simply stunning.

Her little curtsy nearly undid him.

"Captain Navarre," she smiled at him, conveying a wealth of pleasantness.

If he was going to be hung by this woman, at least it would be a nice death.

"Your Grace," he replied with a formal bow.

The others did the same, mostly murmuring.

It was his show. His head.

His vengeance.

"Please," she said, amiable but professional at the same time. "Be seated. What brings you to *Binhai*?"

They were nine around the table, three of the closest chairs remaining empty.

"You asked that we not be enemies, nor strangers," Javier replied, quoting the letter she had sent him after he had broken in and committed a petite vandalism on her starship.

"Indeed," she agreed, fencing ever so exquisitely.

"When last I was here," Javier continued, gesturing to Djamila. "When we were here, it was to do a job for Valko Slavkov."

"I remember," she said lightly. "A most interesting and enlightening adventure was had by all."

Javier let that one go without comment. Not quite the turn of phrase he would have used, but accurate enough, if you wanted to put lipstick on a pig.

"Valko Slavkov apparently was expecting a bloodbath out of everything," Javier replied to her tone. He had feared it would be an effort to not get all growly, impersonating Navarre, but he didn't have to be that guy anymore. Certainly not around her. "He seems to have been rather put out that things turned out so small."

"Yes," the Khatum agreed. "One minor assassination, and even that philosophical and not literal. And the man subsequently escaped with his life and fled on to points unknown. Hopefully you aren't here to finish the job?"

"On the contrary," Javier countered. "Slavkov took the outcome personally enough that he hired one of the Pirate Clans to hunt me down and kill me, along with Captain Sokolov, and his entire crew."

"He seems to have failed," she leaned forward, ever so slightly. If she had chosen to wear something that showed any cleavage at all, any man's eyes would have gone south at that point.

Gods, he missed this sort of repartee.

"He pissed me off." Navarre's tones finally colored the conversation.

"Abram Tamaaz pissed you off, once," she noted dryly, suddenly leaning back in her chair and getting professional again, right at the moment when it had been getting warm and personal.

"Yes," Javier agreed.

She pointed at the horizon over his shoulder.

"Is that what you have planned, with that warship out there?" she inquired.

"Partly," he agreed. "I would like your help, as well."

One perfectly-manicured eyebrow went up exactly the right amount.

Doubt. Sarcasm. Interest. Adventure.

Wow.

"With Captain Sokolov's willing assistance, I'm going after Valko Slavkov, and all his punks," Javier said. "But I'm also going after the people he hired to kill me."

"And who would that be?"

"Walvisbaai Industrial," he replied. "One of the so-called *Pirate Clans.*"

Javier felt the weight of her gaze suddenly shift to his right. To Zakhar.

"As I understand it," she began. "Captain Sokolov happens to belongs to a similar organization."

Zakhar surprised Javier by unfolding his posture from that rigid, military bearing and leaning forward to rest his elbows on the table so he could put his chin on his crossed hands.

"This is personal," Zakhar growled.

Nothing more, but it spoke volumes, coming from a man of such obvious military bearing and reputation.

People were going to die.

And they had it coming.

"I see," she said after a moment of study, her eyes coming back to rest on Javier after pausing to measure both Djamila and Afia. "And my involvement?"

"Piracy is a gray area, Your Grace," Javier purred, all his lessons in maritime law having been recently refreshed as he planned this little escapade. "Law enforcement is not universal, but depends on a variety of jurisdictions. And the *Concord* can't be everywhere. What I have planned could be construed as a capital offense, if committed without prior sanction."

Her eyes got a special glow in them, but she remained silently attentive.

Javier took that as a welcome sign.

"I would like to negotiate a deal with you for *Letters of Marque and Reprisal*," he said simply.

Ninety-nine people in one hundred, the look he would expect back would be blank puzzlement.

Not her. Under all that beauty was a first-class brain, educated way beyond the normal standards for rich aristocrats.

All that, and a bag of chips.

"Elizabeth *Regina* and Francis Drake?" she asked in a tone suddenly bordering on caustic sarcasm.

It took Javier a moment to place the reference.

"Yes, Your Grace," he said. "Just so."

"For how long?" she inquired.

Javier leaned back and thought.

That was the bitch of it.

This might take six months. Or maybe ten years. Luck and timing would play a significant role.

"I believe we can either finish our task, or die trying, inside of two years," he finally settled on.

"Leaving Slavkov dead and Walvisbaai neutered?" she pursued him like a hound after a hare. "What's in it for me?"

Yup. Smart and cunning woman. The best kind.

"Revenge," he said. "Plus plunder. That ship out there is capable of making a serious change to the status quo in a number of places."

"And I should declare open war on your enemies on something so thin?" her tone had turned tart.

Javier nodded. This was where the dickering over brass tacks would get interesting.

"No," she said simply, her dark eyes turning opaque in some way he couldn't describe.

"No?" Javier was mildly stunned. Not at the refusal, but how quickly she got there.

It had always been a possible outcome.

"No," she repeated. "Two years for you, possibly a lifetime of recriminations and potential hostility for me? Simply not worth it. No."

At least she hadn't thrown him out. Hopefully that was a sign.

"What would bring the scales more into balance?" he proffered carefully.

And that's when those black widow's eyes suddenly got lethal.

"Your vessel is a First Rate Galleon, *Neu Berne* style," she observed. "A heavily-armed merchantman, correct?"

Javier nodded cautiously. He hadn't met too many people in his life as dangerous, as smart or cunning, as this woman. This might be the one day where he regretted it.

"If you are to be Drake, there must be voyages of exploration and trade as well," she said simply. "Not just war with Imperial Spain."

"I beg your pardon?" he sputtered.

Javier could feel a stack of history books suddenly piling up on his nightstand. This woman was serious.

"If you want my help," Behnam Sherazi boiled it down tightly. "Then there will be a long-term profit in it for me."

"How long?" Javier asked in a polite voice, aware that he was deep into black widow territory with this woman.

"Let's talk about a ten-year trade partnership, Captain Navarre," she said in a voice that was letting the lethal hardness slowly bleed over into polite warmth. Accounting, rather than vengeance. At least as much as the two differed in this sort of company.

Javier mirrored Zakhar's pose, chin on hands, elbows on the table.

Not the way he had planned it. But maybe there was something in it for everyone, after all. He had always known that this beautiful woman was dangerous.

PART FIVE

JAVIER COULDN'T, for the life of him, think of an event that had left him so emotionally and intellectually wrung out.

Possibly, and this was just a maybe, sitting for his Master Mariner certification, Junior year at the *Bryce Academy*, when they washed out those who were good enough to merely serve, and then separated out the ones who were going to *command*.

He collapsed onto the soft sofa in the luxurious suite she had assigned him, trying not to laugh out loud at the realization that it was the exact same one she had put him in last time, down to the same picture hanging over the bed as in the cheesecake picture she had sent him.

There were rooms for bodyguards he didn't have, with Sykora, Sokolov, and Afia being off in their own rooms. The same three level living room. That same bed in the back room that was big enough to host a small orgy.

He didn't have the energy to even think about it.

At least the woman had spent the five hours of hard negotiation in a polite way, rather than getting brutal about it. And he had a deal.

Of sorts.

It involved naturalizing Javier and all the Centurions of Sokolov's crew as citizens of *Altai*. Subject to her law, on a planet where she was the law. He still had to present it to the crew and see who would balk.

Most of Sokolov's officers were well-enough known in places to have prices on their heads. Being able to come home to a place where they might be safe would probably sway them.

Javier wondered how much of the rest of the crew would take her up on the offer, as well.

Some folks would walk, taking their chances with a fresh start on *Binhai*, or maybe trying to get hired on as part of *Shangdu's* crew. Javier hoped he could make up the difference, the losses, with a quiet recruiting drive.

For what he had in mind, he was probably going to need some retired *Concord* fleet marines. The dangerous kinds.

Fortunately, Djamila Sykora was exactly the person to find them, recruit them, and then qualify them to her high standards. Nobody got to carry a gun around the dragoon without her approval.

Javier eyed the wet bar as he kicked off his shoes and contemplated a nap. He had another three hours before a semi-formal dinner.

The Westminster chimed at the front hatch. Someone wanted to talk.

Javier considered looking. Considered ignoring it. Curiosity won the coin toss.

"Room system, open the hatch," he said.

If someone was here to kill him, they would just have to haul their lazy asses all the way in here to do the job, instead of killing him in the doorway.

Movement in the hallway.

Her.

"Your Grace," Javier said, not even bothering to sit up straighter.

She had changed from the business suit earlier into a navy blue outfit that looked like what you would get if you told an expert fashion designer to drape a tall woman in six meters of silk with a minimum of sewing. It flowed around her like moonlight.

Nobody had any right to look that good after five, long hours of legalisms.

"We're in private," she replied quietly, smiling tightly, as if a shade nervous. *Her?* "You could call me Behnam."

"True," Javier agreed with a tired smile. "But we're also business partners now, to some extent. I'm not sure how appropriate that level of familiarity might be."

"We haven't signed anything yet," she countered. "Until then, you're still just an interesting pirate captain visiting my ship."

Ah ha. Trust this woman to have finely sliced that edge. Hell, it was probably still ethically safe at this point, too.

What she would do to his soul was a whole other conversation.

"Behnam," he finally said aloud. "I was just contemplating some whiskey when you arrived. Would you care to join me?"

"You stay put," she purred with a lively twinkle in her eyes. "Allow me to serve you."

As if those weren't the most dangerous words to ever come out of a woman's mouth.

Still, he gestured for her to proceed and let the arm of the sofa take his weight as he swung his feet up. As nice as the view was, just watching her walk over and grab a pair of highball glasses made him even more tired.

The tinkle of ice sounded a musical note, followed by snaps as she poured the warm, caramel liquid over them.

The sofa was big enough that she could hand him a glass, engulfing him in the glorious floral scent of her perfume, before moving to the far end and settling.

Javier had known cats that couldn't tuck their feet under them so gracefully.

And the way her eyes followed his every movement reminded Javier of an owl waiting on a branch as a clueless rabbit crept out from cover.

"To business," he toasted, raising his glass just a shade.

"Business, yes," she replied.

The first sip of liquid smoke cut through the layer of ice and gunk coating his brain.

It didn't do anything at all to recharge his batteries. Javier suspected that a full nap would be required for that level of human, and she didn't look like that was what she had in mind tonight.

"You really are serious about all this, aren't you?" she finally asked.

"Could you quantify that, please?" he replied in a voice that laid bare all the drain in him.

Thinking was asking too much at this point.

"Revenge," she elaborated. "Destruction. Walvisbaai."

That, however, was the spark to light a fire.

"I didn't choose to become a pirate, Behnam," he said in a voice approximating a bastard sword. Heavy, hard, lethal. "Sokolov captured me and the alternative was a short career as a slave on an agricultural colony somewhere."

"And yet, you're partners, now," she observed. "You trust the man and his crew that much?"

"*Excalibur* is my ship," Javier replied. "He has to trust me."

"You are one man, Eutrupio," she said. "Regardless of how dangerous you might be. What makes you think you're safe?"

Yeah, it was going to be one of those days.

Javier sat more upright and focused his *intent* on the woman at the far end of the galaxy from him.

"Once upon a time, my lady," he began, listening to Navarre's tones color his own. "I had a scout vessel with a *Sentience* as my whole crew. Before *Storm Gauntlet* appeared out of nowhere and killed her. I managed to hide the chips from Zakhar for three years. When I led Sokolov and his crew to the derelict, I poured her into the core. It's hers, now."

"That thing is *Sentient?*" Behnam was shocked. It did lovely things to her eyes.

"She's also my best friend," he said. "The daughter I never had."

"What's she like?" the woman was suddenly concentrating.

"You met her already," Javier said. "That tall, blonde

communications officer you spoke with when we arrived? That's Suvi."

"So if I'm to have a partnership with you, then I'll have one with her as well," Behnam announced. "I'll need to talk to her. Privately. Woman to woman."

Javier fixed her with his best stinkeye, but she was as immune to it as Zakhar seemed to be.

"Fine," he said. "But not this afternoon. I'm so tired I'm not even sure a long soak before whatever it is you have planned for dinner would help."

She smiled. Warm. Friendly. Predatory.

"I could always join you," she said. "Keep you from drowning. Scrub your back. And then maybe snuggle you to sleep."

Even if that hadn't been the best offer he'd gotten in months, Javier wouldn't have turned her down. Lord knew what their relationship would be like once contracts were signed.

He suspected she felt the same.

A last meal for the condemned.

Tomorrow, things were going to get serious.

PART SIX

A NOTE HAD APPEARED in her pocket, as if by magic.

Djamila wasn't sure if she should be aghast that her guard was down that far, or thrilled that he was still that good.

She hadn't been sure how she would approach the man, or the topic. During the conversations with Suvi, back when they first recovered *Hammerfield* from eternity, it had only been a theoretical topic.

Now, she was here. Again. With Zakhar up a deck, presumably resting and preparing for dinner, while she was down in this same dive bar where her adventures on this vessel had begun.

Djamila suddenly felt like a teenager sneaking out after curfew.

Nothing had changed in this room, this bar. She suspected that nothing was ever allowed to change. Continuity for the crew, as they recovered from dealing with rich aristocrat customers that had a tendency to be petulant children.

The lights were just dim enough to let eyes recover, and let minds pretend that there was nobody around, if they got more than two meters away from you.

The bar itself was still tall, with long, gray metal sides and a scarred wooden top, both burned, nicked, and stained with age and character.

An impressive backbar, with exotic bottles four rows high above and a row of meter-tall refrigerators underneath.

Stools all the way around the front, about half of them currently occupied.

That same burly bartender standing behind, with scarred ears and a look like a spring-wakened troll: hungry and mean.

Djamila was still an outsider here. This bar was dedicated to crew, and mostly to engineering-side, rather than service-side. The colors of the uniforms were muted and generally gray.

All the better to disappear when someone in bright tones stepped up to help a lost tourist.

The two stools on the left corner of the bar, along the long axis where it turned in on the short axis, those had not changed. The near corner one was empty, the other was filled.

Farouz.

There were no words to describe the sudden race of emotions, save for the surge of cold adrenaline in her belly.

167 cm tall. Short for a man anywhere, and nearly half a meter shorter than she was.

Wiry. Hard. Carved from steel rods and barbed wire. Covered in skin darker than her tanned bronze. Perhaps Central Asian, like his boss.

Dark hair, cut short and just starting to gray underneath. Clean shaven.

Perfect stillness. Something learned and not natural. Available only to practitioners of deep meditation, or combat arts with meditative elements.

Zen warriors.

She could see him as *Kensei* on the dojo floor, equally at home with katana or bokken.

He moved in ways that very few others did. In her experience, only the most dangerous Special Forces operators could flow like that.

His face was cold, but she felt it warm into a smile as she got close.

The last time she had seen this man, it had been necessary to shoot him. Djamila had only Aritza's word, third-hand, that they had all moved past that ugly incident. That, and a piece of paper with a place and a time. A place she already knew.

He rose as she reached the stool reserved for her, climbed down off his chair as if to emphasize the enormous difference in height. Reached up slowly, one hand going around her hip, the other around her neck to pull her down into a kiss filled with all the promise the last one had.

It was over too soon.

Djamila suspected that they might all be over too soon. But that was the cost of living.

"Thank you," he said, letting go of her soul and returning to his stool.

Djamila took the empty seat next to him.

The bartender smiled and poured something blue into a highball glass unasked, unspoken, and then left with nothing but a wry smile.

So, he remembered her, too.

"I might be recruiting this time," she said, as if the last year had been a day.

"It must be dangerous if you need help," he replied in a low, quiet drawl.

"It will be," she replied with a small smile. "I thought I would get the most dangerous man on this ship to help."

A pause as he studied her. Weighing her soul, perhaps.

They had gone beyond merely comrades, in the space of those two kisses, then and now.

"With you here," Farouz finally said, "I would be fourth most dangerous."

"Fourth?" she was surprised.

"Third would be my teacher," the man observed. "I could not place you second or first against the other person without a head-to-head combat decathlon that would be decided on thousandths of points. But neither of those people would give up their place here. Such are adventures for the young."

From the skin around his neck and his wrists, Djamila

would have guessed him to be in his early forties, perhaps half a decade older than her, but it was hard to tell with a man like that. In this light, he was almost carved from timeless granite.

"And you?" she teased.

"Old enough to know better," he replied with a sudden grin. "Young enough to still do crazy things, like pick up angry Amazons in bars."

Djamila leaned close enough to kiss him again. Because she could.

A year ago, she had been just learning how to be someone other than the *Ballerina of Death*, always at war with Aritza. What was it Javier had said to her, in one of those private conversations?

All possible tomorrows.

"Do you want to know what it is?" she finally asked, breaking the contact and catching her breath from the kiss.

He smiled and raised a glass that had been sitting close. It was also blue.

"It will be a precise aggression," he said, growing cold and serious, but keeping a twinkle in his eyes for her. "Multi-threaded. Relying on stealth and timing. An assassination, of sorts, rather than a frontal assault with overwhelming firepower. Your team will be compact and expert, such that you can rely on professionalism rather than long experience with a teammate and thus allowing you to recruit outside your immediate crew."

Djamila remembered to pick her jaw up and close her mouth before she caught any flies.

"Any other option would require six months of training," Farouz continued. "And Captain Navarre does not strike me as that type, from my experience with the man and his methods."

"No, you are absolutely right," Djamila confessed. "Navarre is after revenge on the man who sent us here originally, for a double-cross later."

"And you, Hadiiye?" Farouz probed. "What do you seek?"

"I have another name," she hesitated.

"So do we all," he countered, still smiling. "Hadiiye was the one I wanted. Not whoever that woman was when she went back to her other life. That other woman was not happy, with herself or her situation. Hadiiye had hope."

"And she still does," the woman whispered, unsure exactly who she was right now as the roles began to bleed into one another.

Djamila considered the advice of Dr. Wilhelmina Teague. And Suvi. And even Afia Burakgazi. All women that had tried to help her overcome herself.

"We want to be free," she finally whispered.

Farouz nodded.

"Then show me who we need to kill to free you," he said.

BOOK TWENTY-TWO: NEMESIS

PART ONE

T HIS WAS the point when Zakhar felt a twinge of regret.

Only a twinge, mind you, tempered greatly by the feeling of immense security that he got from being surrounded by a warship of this scale and raw power.

But a little regret, nonetheless.

Storm Gauntlet had been a low-profile corvette to begin with. A tiny little escort turned sneaky. On top of that, his bosses had layered on a stealth cloak good enough to hide them from most sensor systems until he was right on top of someone and they had to spot him visually.

For a pirate, the best way to catch prey. Like one Mr. Javier Aritza.

That wasn't an option with this mighty kraken, this First Rate Galleon. This thing called *Hammerfield*.

Javier and Suvi had decided to rename this ship as *Excalibur*, for reasons generally lost on him, but an inside joke with a number of the crew members, including Djamila.

Zakhar supposed he could ask her, or Suvi. He could even look it up, if he thought it mattered all that much. Maybe tomorrow. It must be good to elicit the kinds of giggles it had.

Everyone else in orbit had hard-pinged them when *Excalibur* got close enough to orbit to register on their scans as something new and impressive. Well, old and even more impressive. They didn't make warships like these any more.

Today, the ship was sitting in a medium orbit of *Merankorr*, a planet mostly famous for its brothels and orbital foundries but also home to two of the best shipyards in space. Soon, they would be granted a docking assignment and could unload their cargo.

Zakhar would shed a few tears when they were done. It was the nature of things.

He would miss his old bridge.

Excalibur had an enormous command space, a round room about twenty-seven meters across, with a domed ceiling 9.2 meters at the peak. Him ensconced atop a pedestal at the center, surrounded by stations for six Centurions and twelve more crew. You could set up a volleyball net in here and hold tournaments.

At least the crew had painted everything an earthy brown to replace the stark, gunmetal gray it had been. Warmer. Homier.

And enough different from the first time he had boarded, with Captain Mayer's corpse still seated in this very chair, that Zakhar didn't think he would have too many zombie nightmares.

Hopefully, Mayer's ghost approved of everything they were doing.

Zakhar didn't need to sit a duty watch on the bridge. Probably shouldn't. There was always paperwork that needed doing. Less than before, with Suvi handling things, but some.

At the same time, it kept his head in the game.

He had known commanders that never did this. Never spent four hours on the bridge so all the other centurions could have some downtime. Never interacted directly with the enlisted crew who were the rugged backbone of any good ship.

Those captains frequently weren't his favorites. Or Fleet's.

Even on a warship of this immense scale, it was possible to have a small crew. He needed to know everyone, and know them well.

Technically, he could go with a crew even smaller than *Storm Gauntlet* had required, but he would need to recruit a larger ground combat contingent one of these days. Assuming they stayed in the piracy business.

With this much firepower and cargo capacity at hand, all sorts of other options presented themselves as well. Not that he wanted to become a warlord/God-Emperor of some little backwards planet out in the sticks, but he could. Assuming Javier and Suvi wanted to.

Or he could get serious about just hauling cargo for a living. Boring and safe, but profitable. Again, what would Javier and Suvi think? Or Djamila?

"Captain, we have an update," Suvi's warm voice filled the room, breaking him out of the dark place his thoughts were heading.

"Go ahead, Suvi," he replied.

"We are next in the queue for the dry-dock, sir," Suvi said. "Estimated time to dock is two to three hours."

"Acknowledge them, please, and let Afia and Andreea know," he ordered.

Down below, what was left of *Storm Gauntlet*'s corpse was blind, toothless, and naked, stowed in the aft-most primary cargo bay. With time available and dedicated crew, Chief Engineer Andreea Dalca and Afia Burakgazi had removed every sensor and weapon from the little corvette, as well as the cloak generator. Then they stripped it of every useful bit of anything they could, since they had space to stow the results.

The ship's name plate, formerly welded to the aft bulkhead on the bridge, had been cut off and put in Zakhar's personal cabin as a memento. Right before every single identifying transmitter and ID number had been wiped, removed, or etched off with an angle grinder.

They had even split her shell into three big pieces, making it easier to remove Javier's arboretum and shift it into the forward-most bay over here, several decks directly below him, which was then sealed off and turned into something of a park for the crew.

What was left were piles of metal and parts. The badly damaged corpse of a *Concord* corvette, unidentifiable, except by process of elimination of any such private vessels still in service somewhere. And there were enough of those to mask which one this was.

He would miss her, to be sure, but he had *Hammerfield/Excalibur* now.

Trading up for bigger problems.

Shortly, a tiny, little superrunt of a tug would come alongside to nudge them into alignment with the dry-dock and guide them in. Ship's gravity would be turned entirely off for half a day while every available crew member with EVA certifications helped the shipyard crew to move the corvette's body over, under Afia's supervision. Her soul would remain behind with the crew.

They would make a good chunk of money from this deal.

And all of this was just a cover to get close enough to their target to be able to scan it at close range with nobody the wiser. With the sorts of sensor capabilities originally taken off of a retired *Concord* probe-cutter, and subsequently reprogrammed by a highly-competent Science Officer-turned-pirate.

Who was himself leading a very dedicated, very angry group of people, Zakhar included.

Valko Slavkov had no idea what he had awakened.

Today's target was a freighter. Of a sort.

Zakhar had been deeply impressed by the *Land Leviathan*, that enormous, tracked resort vehicle. A desert train with ten massive cars, each sixty meters on a side and thirty tall, with big treads waddling slowly across whatever world Slavkov owned or rented.

He knew Aritza had been plotting how to steal the thing since the first time the two of them had seen it.

For Zakhar, it was the engineering feat to move the Leviathan between worlds that engaged his dreams. He had originally expected that each of the ten cars was hauled to orbit individually and then stowed aboard a megafreighter. A monster even bigger than the kraken that was *Excalibur*, big enough to ensnare the ship, but not nearly as heavily armed.

The truth was even more surprising. A ship in the form of

an isosceles trapezoid with a narrow width at the bow, wider at the stern, and long in the body, with two massive, squat engines thrust off the back like stubby legs, like the Cyrillic capital letter *De. Д.* The whole reminded him of something like a dachshund hound.

Nothing much to look at, until you realized that the whole ship was completely hollow, with everything contained in the outer walls. The space in the middle, coming up from between the engine wells, seven hundred meters long, was where the pilot would drive the entire beast of the Land Leviathan, once the lander was on the ground. Giant waldoes came out of the sides at that point and clamped onto the Leviathan to secure it into place, and then the ship would slowly take off and move to orbit, where it would rendezvous with its escorts and head off to the next destination.

The carrier ship that was off their starboard bow right now, slowly finishing up a refit before heading off to the next mission.

The next desert world, probably.

Zakhar figured that someone like Valko Slavkov, a bully born rich, probably didn't travel with the bigger vessel, but would spend some time visiting someone else's fairy castle while his moved to a new location.

What must it be like to have so much wealth that you could do things like that for fun?

Zakhar was fourth generation *Concord* fleet. Second as an officer. Quite possibly the last, unless circumstances changed in the next few years and he finally got serious about having a family.

Nobody got rich in the service. Well, the bankers did, same as with pirates.

Even selling off the shattered remains of *Storm Gauntlet* wouldn't really make him rich. Javier was getting a quarter, Zakhar and the crew was getting another quarter according to a complicated formula, and a quarter went to their new investor/business partner. The *Khatum of Altai.* The last slice was going into a ship's maintenance fund.

It would keep *Excalibur* in socks and fresh cream for maybe a decade, if they were frugal.

And lucky enough to survive that long. But first, he and Javier had to see a man about a horse.

———

"CAPTAIN," the voice came out of a speaker on his desk. "I'd really appreciate you down in the cargo bay, please."

Zakhar's head snapped up.

Afia never did that. She was among the most self-contained engineers--hell, people--he knew. Utterly competent and happy to take care of things herself.

That was why he had put her in charge of this task. That, and she was gregarious enough to work with dock teams, whereas his chief engineer was a barely-functioning introvert who was happier down with her generators and engines.

Afia didn't ask for help unless it was bad. Or getting there quickly. She had a good eye for that sort of thing, too. And she must have been around civilians, so she didn't want to say "NOW" but he could read between the lines.

"Be along shortly," he keyed the comm, already rising from the seat in his day office and moving towards the hatch.

They hadn't shut down the gravplates yet, so the task took longer. In freefall, he could have basically swam there in a few powerful kicks, bouncing off walls and plates as he went.

Even at fifty-five, he could still out-maneuver anybody in this crew, excepting only Djamila.

Nope, he pounded down stairs like his ass was on fire today. Through the hatch and into the grand mausoleum that held his last command.

Afia was there, along with a group of *Concord* officers.

Made sense. *Storm Gauntlet* was a retired *Concord* warship. *Merankorr* was a *Concord* world. And Zakhar had every damned one of their forms and certificates properly filled out, the benefit of the *Khatum's* legal affairs officers very carefully doing their job.

As he got close to the group, Zakhar blinked and nearly stutter-stepped, but he swallowed his reaction before it got to his face.

Only the eyes maybe showed anything.

Reflected in the face of the main guy over there, just turning away from his conversation with Afia to look this direction. The man with four solid yellow rings on each wrist, plus a broken one above that. In a uniform that was the origin of the green suit Zakhar wore as a rule.

A guy Zakhar knew.

Crap.

"Captain Zakhar Sokolov," he said loudly, forcefully as he got within polite range, drawing everyone in the area into his orbit by sheer force of will. He was good at that. Even Javier listened, most of the time. "Is there a problem?"

There was, but Zakhar wasn't going to admit it first.

"Commodore Nguyên Ayokunle," the stranger in charge of the other group replied as he turned and flinched, ever so slightly. "No problem, Captain. Since your cargo is military hardware, disposal falls under my purview. Plus, your vessel caught my attention."

Yeah, it would. History had always been your thing, hadn't it, Yên?

Old memories flooded back, but Zakhar kept his face neutral.

"How so?" Zakhar decided to play stupid, just in case.

The man was tall and skinny, with dark brown skin and fluffy ringlets gone totally white.

Another reason Zakhar kept his own head shaved at all times.

Commodore was a courtesy rank. Senior captain assigned to a system or task force that didn't rate an Admiral, at a time when budget cut backs meant fewer and fewer flag slots available.

One of the primary reasons Zakhar had left the straight and narrow. And why he had so many competent people to crew with.

Yên smiled at him in a calculating way.

"*Station Sentience* flagged you as a *Neu Berne*-style Galleon," the commodore replied in a questioning tone. "That's a lot of firepower for a private-service vessel. And this is a very old ship that doesn't appear anywhere in our records."

"We salvaged a derelict," Zakhar replied evenly. It was even the truth. "And we frequently have to operate in places folks like you never go."

Leave it at that. Do not poke a sleeping bear with anything less than a very long stick.

"And flagged out of *Altai*," Yên continued the thought. "That's a long ways away."

"I just work here," Zakhar decided to go shallow and stupid on the man. Hell, it might even work if this very senior *Concord* officer chose to play along.

"Who owns this ship?" Yên asked pointedly.

Around them, the *Concord* folks were getting the least bit twitchy. Afia, too.

But this was EXACTLY why he and Javier had spent so much time on their cover story and all the paperwork to back it up.

"Corporate chain," Zakhar said. "Like a nautilus shell. Built in layers that run all over the place. I do know that the *Khatum of Altai* herself was a major investor."

Along with me, Javier, and a crew committee represented by the tiny, Indonesian woman to my immediate right, but you don't need to know that, Yên.

"I see," Yên observed in a tone so dry Zakhar needed a glass of water. "Have we met somewhere? You look familiar."

I dunno. The guy who tutored you through Orbital Mechanics II? Who might have ended up your brother-in-law, if your sister hadn't decided she wanted to marry a stay-at-home accountant instead of a fleet officer?

Have we met?

"I get that a lot," Zakhar replied in a carefully bored tone. "Had a cousin who was in the navy who looks a lot like me. You might have known him."

Yên nodded silently.

"And your cargo?" Yên said. "Manifest ranks it as a *Concord* corvette, demilitarized and stripped."

The commodore gestured at the metal art installations behind them. A proud corpse in three big pieces and hundreds of little ones. Nobody had bothered to buff out the scorch marks and damage *Ajax* had done before the wee Viking longboat had slipped away at *Svalbard*.

"My understanding?" Zakhar said with a shrug. "Story goes that she was a pirate who got more than she bargained for. Escaped by the skin of her teeth, but it wasn't economical to repair her, so a stripper crew dismantled her and we're hauling the lot here to *Merankorr* for the foundry. Lot of good metal here that just needs to be recast into a new ship."

Zakhar could see the list of questions Yên wanted to ask, but not in front of this many witnesses. Zakhar felt the same way.

How often do you suddenly run into a man who was your best friend forty years ago, whom you haven't seen in at least fifteen?

"Interesting," Yên replied. "Where are you headed from here?"

"*Purton*," Zakhar lied easily. That was in the paperwork already. "Dead-heading to get a load to haul to *Meehu*."

"Dangerous places," Yên agreed. "Good thing you have all this firepower to protect you. Likely to be back through *Merankorr* anytime soon?"

Zakhar shrugged.

"They wouldn't be such bad places if you folks did your jobs more," Zakhar said, unable to resist the dig. And maybe reflect a little of the anger Zakhar had at where their two distinct lives had ended up.

Yên bristled. Just a bit.

The *Concord* was still recovering from the time and expense spent cleaning up nearly a century of war and strife caused by other people, but Zakhar knew they had cut too much, too soon, even after two generations of relative peace.

Too many worlds were still left on their own. Too much

military hardware like this First-Rate-Galleon floating around, just waiting for a sociopath who wanted to make himself a petty god.

Zakhar was sure Yên would have savagely dressed down a civilian who mocked him like that that in public, even on the safety of his own deck.

Zakhar watched the man clench his jaws, grinding his teeth rather than lash out.

The moment of rage passed.

Zakhar watched all the *Concord* officers relax as their boss did. Afia had been remarkably silent and unobtrusive through the whole thing, but Zakhar recognized her stance as a small woman sizing a bigger man up for a swift kick to the balls in a sudden fight.

"Captain Sokolov," Yên nodded professionally. "Maybe next time you're in-system we'll have more time to chat."

"I look forward to that, Commodore," Zakhar said.

The chances of ever being this deep in *Concord* space again were awful slim, especially after *Excalibur* got a reputation for what they were about to do next.

And if they did, Zakhar would be expecting a heavily-armed warship, maybe even a *Warmaster*, to be orbiting in close proximity, all guns aimed and twitchy.

Neither of them would be fooling around at that point.

DELRIDGE SMITH DIDN'T REALLY LIKE to play the part of grumpy, old man. Took too much effort most days, like shaving. Sure, he had old down. Weren't many pilots in their seventh decade still flying combat missions. But he preferred his comfy, gray pants with the thigh pockets, and his collection of Hawaiian shirts. And his flight deck on *Excalibur's* nameless assault shuttle, all pink fur and glitter paint.

Soothed a man.

Weren't soothed right now, sitting in his piloting station, turned around facing backwards.

Del gave up and let a little growl loose in the direction of his visitor.

Javier Aritza. Still technically the ship's science officer, but that was while everyone was sorting out this new life aboard a *Sentient* warship who was kinda a goof.

The good kind. Del's kind.

Her, not Javier.

"Zakhar tells me you aren't thrilled with the modifications," Javier said judiciously.

He was a shade taller than Del. And in much better shape. Still didn't want to poke a grumpy old man. Good for him.

"Bucko, if I'd wanted to fly like that, I would'a retired and gotten a job as a chauffeur for dumbass admirals," Del fired back. "Calm, casual, polite? What the hell kind of fun is that?"

"Most people would enjoy having enough cloak on their shuttle as to be invisible, you know, Del," Javier said.

"You think I'd look good in a cute, little cap, bub?" Del nearly snarled.

Give Javier credit. He at least smiled in commiseration.

"We don't have time to steal, buy, or build something else, Del," Javier replied. "But if you feel that way, I got two options for you."

"Shoot."

"One, I promise you we'll only do it once, and then strip everything," Javier smiled evilly.

"And two?" Del asked.

"We could always recruit a second pilot when we do acquire a cloaked shuttle," Javier said. "And let him fly us when we need stealth insertions."

Del felt his eyes narrow. If he was a snake, now would have been the point his eyes slitted up hard vertically, too. Javier didn't make threats. And that was a threat.

Felt like maybe Del'd pushed the man far enough today.

"It's unnatural, flying like that," Del finally huffed, knowing he'd lost this round. "Too boring."

Javier nodded.

"We can always get you a combat fighter," he said. "Little snub-nose, one-man attack ship. If we end up going into the cargo business, we're going to need a big cargo lighter to haul stuff to and from orbit. Pretty boring, though."

"Q-ship it," Del said. "This shuttle as a heavily-armed freighter. Add a couple of pop-up turrets in back and I'll fly all the cargo runs you want. Then you can put some dumbass kid in a fighter, and buy him a cute shuttle to haul admirals around in, too."

"I'll see what I can do," Javier said, turning to leave. "We good?"

"Yes," Del grumbled.

Javier had called his bluff. And he was bluffing. Flying

admirals or containers around was about all the job he could get, these days. Best to stick with the folks who let him keep the craziness in the cockpit.

"Thank you, Del," Javier said as he headed down the stairs to the cargo deck.

Del nodded at the back of the man's head. His part of the coming mission was a piece of cake. Boring. Easy enough that any dumbass kid fresh from flight school could do it.

Javier was going to owe him, after this.

PART THREE

AFTER ALL THESE YEARS, Djamila still had no idea who Hogan was. Or why a combat training simulation like this was named after him. And why it was Hogan's Alley and not Street or something. She had just needed to burn off angry energy.

Looking up at the monitor as she finished the run, her score had been atrocious, by her standards. Barely ahead of any of her men. Probably the worst score Djamila had put up in three years.

She just wasn't sure who she was, anymore.

Once upon a time, she had been the most dangerous woman to ever receive her Combat EVA certifications from the *Neu Berne Navy*. The *Ballerina of Death*, a name she had earned for her ability to use two pistols simultaneously on different targets in zero-grav combat maneuvers.

Javier still muttered under his breath that she must actively worship a death goddess to be that good. She didn't, but Aritza had no idea what made a woman like her tick.

No, her only competition was perfection. And she wasn't there today. She was back in that other place. The dark place.

One day, she had been the best there was wearing the gray uniform. The next, done. Demobilized. Demilitarized.

Civilian.

Djamila knew she had been circling the drain, psychologically, at that moment when someone had introduced her to Zakhar Sokolov, the man who had given her purpose. Place.

Respect.

Everything had been easier, then. Straightforward. Predictable.

And then Javier Aritza happened to her.

For the more-than-two-years since that day, they'd both silently committed to a personal war that drove them both to be better. Unwritten rules in a duel to the death.

Along the way, Dr. Teague had opened Djamila's mind up to other ways of thinking, living. Helped her become more of a person, and less of a cardboard cutout popping up on a Hogan's Alley to kill or be killed.

And then *Shangdu*. The starship known as the Pleasure Dome.

Farouz.

Djamila might be willing to admit, to herself only, her crush on Captain Sokolov. The feelings she thought were reciprocated, but could never ask.

Not the *captain*.

And at *Shangdu*, she had met someone who happily appreciated her as a dangerous creature, but not one he had to compete with. Who didn't demand anything from her at all. Something she had never known before.

A dangerous man who was willing to walk a step behind her, if necessary, because he knew how troubled she was. To remain at arm's length, rather than walk away when she wouldn't let him any closer.

She had kissed him four times. All of them aboard *Shangdu*, the first separated from the others by a year. And not once since. Even though he was on this ship with her now. Somewhere on *Excalibur*.

Kissable.

Djamila told herself that they were in OpSec. Operational

Security mode. Mission imminent. Time to focus. No time for emotional entanglements.

That was a lie.

She was a coward, underneath.

Looking at the monitor board, at the terrible score she had just posted, just shared with the world, she had to admit the truth. Whisper it, at least, since she doubted anyone else would have the audacity to point out how bad she had done. The best of her team might challenge that score on an exceptional day.

Unacceptable.

Djamila turned away from the hallway that was Hogan's Alley and faced the door to the rest of the ship. She sat her disarmed weapons on the training rack for cleaning and recharge later and pressed the big, blue button that deactivated the Alley.

Made it safe for others.

Opened it up for someone to come in and actually compete with her numbers.

She watched the hatch slide open then exited the combat range, passing into the locker room beyond and letting the panel slide shut behind her, desperately afraid that her failure was written on her face.

Hopefully, she could shower and escape before anyone could come along and point out how far she had fallen.

Afia Burakgazi was waiting for her, seated on the old, wooden bench that ran between the tall rows of faded-mustard yellow, metal lockers.

Djamila couldn't help herself. The sight of the tiny engineer, with such a serious face, brought her to a halt.

"Sit," the woman commanded.

Djamila felt her feet betray her by obeying.

Seated, the woman came up to her shoulder, but that was normal. As females went, Djamila had always been long-torsoed to go with her long legs. Built more like a man that way.

Today, it just reinforced the supreme distance between the two of them.

Afia watched her silently for a few moments, as if reading her mind.

"Yeah," the engineer said in a quiet voice. "She was right."

"Who?" Djamila said before she could slam her jaws shut to swallow the words.

Escaped horses and barn doors.

"Suvi," Afia replied. "She said you looked like someone who needed to talk, but she wouldn't tell me anything more than that."

Djamila felt her eyes narrow.

Suvi knew more of the truth than anyone, the benefit of being invisible and able to watch people for several years. The *Sentience* knew too many of Djamila's secrets.

Hopefully, it was a good sign that the *Sentience* had asked the engineer to help. Afia wasn't a gossip.

"Watched you in the run, just now," Afia began deliberately. "I might have done better."

Djamila actually flinched under the words. Her, the iron maiden who was impervious to all things. How far had she fallen? How quickly?

"A word of advice?" Afia continued. "Don't ever play poker with anybody, okay?"

"What?" Djamila was confused by the sudden change. "Why not?"

"Because poker is a mental game, an emotional one," Afia replied. "You win by reading the other players around the table and understanding what they know and don't know by simple body language. And by not letting them know you. The very best players can actually lie to you at the table with nothing but the set of their eyes or the way they hold their hands with the cards. You begin to believe what they are about to do, and they trick you."

The tiny engineer fell silent and watched her.

Djamila felt like a teenage girl again, being reprimanded by her mother for something. She even blushed.

"Yes," Afia said. "That. A good player suppresses that. A

great player fakes it. I would take all your money very quickly if we were to play."

Another awkward silence. Djamila felt the ground open under her feet, leaving a precarious ledge in high winds, welcoming her into the abyss.

"Here's a really tough question, Djamila," Afia said. "And it might help. Which man do you love more?"

Djamila felt all the air rush out of her lungs. Her chest seemed to collapse in on itself.

Silence.

Afia seemed content to wait.

Djamila felt herself tear into two separate pieces inside.

The *Dragoon, Warrior Princess* of *Storm Gauntlet* and now *Excalibur.* The lethal right arm of Captain Sokolov, forever at his side and never destined to be with him.

Or *Hadiiye*, the dangerous assassin who was the bodyguard to Captain Navarre and moved like a golden lioness, proud and lethal, but softer. More *flexible.* The woman who had kissed Farouz and considered what it would be like to take the man to bed for a good, long romp.

"I can't choose." The words forced themselves out of her mouth.

Djamila blushed even harder at the revelation of her darkest secret.

"Why do you have to?" Afia asked simply.

"What?"

The tiny woman could have pushed her over with a feather.

"You could have them both, you know," the engineer said.

"How is that possible?" Djamila whispered.

"Look at the rest of us," Afia grinned. "All of us have Javier, and none of us. We share, but nobody has his heart. That doesn't stop us from enjoying ourselves occasionally. There's nothing stopping you from having both men."

"But he's the captain," she replied fiercely, even if her voice remained tiny.

"So?"

Djamila didn't think she had ever heard someone pack so much depth and meaning into a single syllable.

"What do you mean?" Djamila asked.

"So he's the captain," Afia said. "Did he take a vow of chastity or something?"

"Well, no," Djamila agreed. "But that's not how it works in the service. In any service."

"Can I let you in on a secret, Djamila?" Afia continued. "We're not in the navy any more. Any of us. We're private contractors doing a service industry transportation job. The only thing stopping you from doing anything is yourself. And probably him. Plus, he is the captain, so he'd be feeling too guilty, like he was taking advantage of you."

"And Farouz?" Djamila asked, wonder slowly creeping into her tones as the implications of Afia's words slithered into her mind. Was it possible?

"You gonna marry that boy? Go set up a dojo somewhere and pop out crazy, little, ninja babies?"

The image made Djamila burst out laughing in spite of herself. Laughing felt good. Cathartic. Liberating.

Afia joined in after a moment.

It took several minutes of joy for Djamila to bring herself back to center.

A center she had almost forgotten existed.

"No," Djamila finally managed, after she had gotten the giggles stuffed back into a box. "I don't see Farouz and I settling down on a planet. Too boring."

"Good," Afia agreed. "Now, when was the last time you got laid?"

Djamila felt the blush simply explode, painting her like a rotten tomato as she crimsoned as far down her chest as one could.

"A while," she stammered, catching her breath.

"How many years?" Afia stalked her relentlessly, eyes glittering like a cat suddenly revealed in the light.

"Seven," Djamila admitted, back down to her tiny voice.

Afia's eyes got big, and then friendlier. Warmer.

"Then you need to head up to his cabin right now, or wherever he is, and do something about that," Afia pronounced.

"Now?"

Djamila was horrified. Spinning. Knocked right back off that center she had just regained. She started to rise, but Afia caught her by the arm, let her miniscule weight anchor Djamila's butt to the warm, wooden bench.

"I can't," Djamila pled with her captor. "I need a shower. I need time to prepare."

"If I gave you any time, you'd talk yourself out of it, Djamila."

Afia's voice had turned to pure doom at this point, a dagger penetrating her mind relentlessly.

"What are you saying?" Djamila asked.

"Come with me."

Afia took her hand and rose, dragging Djamila to her feet, all 2.1 meters of sweaty dragoon, rank and smelly.

The engineer's hand was like a manacle on her wrist as they moved.

At the hatch to the main corridor, Afia switched to holding her hand like young lovers on a third date, but Djamila wasn't fooled. Afia was willing to drag her kicking and screaming if necessary.

At the same time, a small voice in the back of Djamila's head pointed out how much bigger she was than the other woman. How much stronger. How easy it would be to plant her feet and simply say no.

If she really wanted to.

And that was the gulf. That hollow space surrounding her.

Djamila wasn't about to walk across that bridge. Afia was going to metaphorically drag her.

And both women knew that Djamila would let her.

An elevator opened. Afia pulled her in.

"Deck four, please," Afia said to the open air.

"Coming up," Suvi replied as the elevator started to move.

Suvi.

Afia had been sent on this mission because Suvi knew the

truth but would not betray Djamila's secrets. And Afia was willing to help her friend on nothing more than that.

Was that what it meant to have friends?

Djamila racked her brain, and couldn't remember any friends after the first semester of training school. Everyone else had become competition for the few slots at the top of the class.

And she had chosen to beat them all by walling them off from her and turning into the *Ballerina of Death*.

In twenty-two years, had she never had a friend? And yet, right now, she had at least two people willing to go out of their way to aid her. Help her get over herself.

The hatch opened. Afia's grip had not lessened one iota. Her short legs churned as she dragged the taller woman along the main corridor forward.

Afia finally stopped at the door that had been Captain Mayer's cabin, once upon a time.

Captain Sokolov's now.

Zakhar.

With her free hand, Afia pushed the ringer.

Sokolov answered quickly.

"Come," he said in that warm, authoritarian baritone that triggered all the happy places in Djamila's brain.

Afia went through first as the hatch opened, pulling Djamila behind her.

The front room was a salon, designed for semi-formal meetings with a round, cherry-stained oak table capable of seating six comfortably in stiff, matching chairs.

The art was designed to look professional, rather than personal. Military themes, but historical, with men on horses or foot, wielding swords and pistols. Not what one would expect from a naval officer, but Djamila didn't know what kind of man Captain Mayer had been, and his personal logs had not been a topic she had taken the time to investigate.

She made a promise to know the man better, starting tomorrow.

Right now, she found herself in the middle of a bridge that a petite engineer seemed intent on burning behind her.

She looked up and found Zakhar standing just at the inner door, the one that led to a more cozy salon for entertaining informally. Somewhere beyond that, the man's office and personal quarters.

He had a look of amused confusion on his face when Djamila turned to him.

"Ladies," he temporized. "What can I do for you?"

Afia took a half step forward.

"This woman needs to talk to you," she said, emphasizing the hand that had drug Djamila this far. "Having delivered her, I'm going to leave."

Djamila felt almost naked when Afia released her hand and quickly departed. Suvi must have been watching as well, because the hatch opened and closed without any delay.

Djamila was alone with him.

Zakhar.

She swallowed past a lump in her throat that threatened to strangle her.

Zakhar was wearing blue slacks today, with a black pullover shirt.

She could only see him in her mind wearing *Concord* green, but then she realized that in the week since they had left *Merankorr*, he had not worn green once.

As if he was striving to become somebody else.

Too.

He watched her patiently. He would. He was a very patient man.

Djamila felt the tide start to recede around her, threatening to ground her on hostile rocks. Her palms were suddenly sweaty and clammy. Her pulse threatened to make her head explode.

She fought it all down. Found that center she had when laughing with Afia. That freedom.

Djamila Sykora, dragoon, took a deep breath and held it.

Released it.

Found her voice.

"I'm told that I needed to come see you," she said quietly, almost diffidently. "Told by friends I didn't even know I had."

"I see," Zakhar said, still not quite sure what to make of the woman in front of him, obviously. "Sit down then, please. What is it you wanted?"

The ledge. The cliff. The darkness below her opened up.

"You," she whispered.

He blinked.

Blinked again.

Djamila felt her heart stop, felt that cold, savage burst of adrenaline flood her belly.

Zakhar would grow angry now.

Would cast her down from the heavens for her impertinence.

Her career, her life, was over.

Done.

Goodbye.

Would she take the blade, or just walk off a cliff?

The silence stretched.

And then he smiled.

And held out a hand.

And all the weight in the universe vanished from her shoulders.

BOOK TWENTY-THREE: LEVIATHAN

PART ONE

Javier had decided to spend most of his time the past few days down on the cargo deck of the nameless assault shuttle, rather than up on the bridge with Del. There was a limit to the amount of under-the-breath grumbling he was willing to tolerate, even from his favorite pilot.

And Del would be bitching.

Hammerfield had dropped out of the last jump clear out on the very edge of this system. So far away that it had taken the shuttle three days of high-speed run to get to the third planet, a mostly uninhabited place known as *Alkonost*. Three days of quiet autopilot accelerating them in, and then decelerating them to orbit, all alone from what they could detect.

Even with the pictures taken from orbit, Javier could tell why the place was largely uninhabited. Most worlds were blue and white from space. This one was brown. Too much dust in the air, not enough water to rain it back down. Three monstrous continents dominating a handful of small, relatively-shallow oceans. Terraforming had been successful, but the result was still ugly, combined with the ancient tectonics that had shaped the planet's bones.

According to the *Concord Gazetteer*, vast swaths of steppe

grass fed huge herds of semi-feral cattle, thriving in a place with no large predators. In between, running about twenty degrees of latitude centered more or less on the equator, a desert belt circled nearly three-quarters of the planet, running from one sea to another across the spine of the two biggest continents.

Javier could imagine that there were lovely beaches to be had, if you looked hard enough. White sand, tropical warmth without all the nasty humidity, good surf. But the nightlife would be utterly boring.

He had never been to the fabled California Coast, back on the Homeworld, but this could have been twelve thousand kilometers of competition, on the western shore here.

And that jackass wanted to drive his tank over the sand.

Javier wondered if Del's grumbles were contagious.

The cargo bay on the assault shuttle wasn't designed as a personnel carrier. Sure, there were two heads and a shower section, but no private bunks to retire to when you wanted to avoid people.

And Javier was really getting tired of people, even as tiny as this assault force had finally ended up.

Sykora had brought her six men, the ones Javier liked to refer to as the gun-bunnies, since they were all dedicated soldiers who liked to think of themselves as true warriors. He'd never even bothered to really get to know any of them, since they acted like dumbass, juvenile grunts most of the time.

Djamila was in tactical command. There wasn't anybody he knew better qualified for that role. And he was pretty sure he didn't have to worry about getting shot in the back any more, either by calculated intent or when the woman just finally disintegrated psychologically and started shooting.

Apparently, he had Afia to thank, but he had very carefully chosen to not ask the details. If he hadn't known any better, Javier would have said that the tall woman had finally got laid, there was that big a change in her outlook.

She was relaxed, calm, copacetic. She even smiled occasionally.

Frightening.

Maybe it was Farouz. Sykora had been mopey for nearly a month after she had shot the man, a year ago, but they both seemed to be completely comfortable today.

And the rest of the team was gelling as well.

Djamila had brought her two pathfinders on this mission: Sascha Koç, the short, Slavic brunette with nice hips; and Hajna Flores, the lanky, Anglo blond with forever legs.

Sascha had even largely gotten over the betrayal that Javier had pulled on her, on everyone, to get Suvi installed on *Hammerfield* when nobody was looking. These days, when she threatened to shoot him, she was mostly kidding.

Hajna had missed all that excitement at the time, so her relationship with him hadn't gone through any ugly recriminations. Well, any more than normal. She was a very complex woman who wasn't sure what she wanted out of life.

Javier could commiserate. He generally preferred to not have to grow up and act like management, regardless of circumstances.

Afia rounded out the command group from *Hammerfield*. She was still the best combat EVA engineer he knew, and was willing to go on crazy adventures with one pistol and a tool belt full of wrenches. This foray would probably need both.

Those eleven, Javier at least knew well enough to trust. It was the last two that made him nervous.

He didn't care that both Farouz and Sykora had vouched for them. Of the whole crew, only Del had ever been in places as comparably crazy as Javier.

Rence Moore. A petite, Hispanic woman, late twenties, no bigger than Afia for size, but a skeleton of hard muscles who never smiled.

If Djamila was a soldier's soldier, and Sascha and Hajna were scouts, this one was an assassin.

Dress it up any pretty way you wanted, but Javier had seen that look in her eyes over coffee yesterday morning. He liked to joke about the black widows he had known, but it had always been a joke up until now.

Rence wasn't joking.

And if she represented darkness, the final member of the team was probably *Light*. Gerey 'Spider' Fernandez was a long, lanky dork of an Anglo that Farouz had introduced originally as a *vertical penetrations expert*.

Javier had no idea why the *Khatum* had a professional cat burglar on her staff, or if she even understood what that man was, under that blond *bon homie* and constant smile. Grandma would have called him a harmless surfer punk. She would have been wrong.

Right now, he was practicing his art by free climbing the cargo bay. Up one wall, and right now halfway across the ceiling, dangling from a coolant pipe as he worked his way around a power conduit that wouldn't hold his weight.

If Rence always wore dark clothing that encapsulated her and blurred her outlines, like any good ninja, Spider was wearing a pair of long, fluorescent green and yellow shorts and a faded black, concert t-shirt for a band Javier had never heard of. The only thing that marked him as serious were the extremely light climbing shoes he had on and the weird gloves that pretty much only covered the backs of his hands, leaving the palm open and wrapping just around the base of all his fingers.

And he could traverse the entire ceiling without ever touching the deck.

Javier knew they were all pros, but right now, he wanted a quiet corner with walls he could go hide behind. Four days in these people's pockets was pushing it.

"Javier," Del's growl came over the intercom. "We're about there."

"Coming," he called back, grateful for the opportunity to do something.

Up on the bridge, the view was spectacular.

For no reason whatsoever, as far as Javier could tell, the shuttle was flying upside down, relative to the planet, leaving him hanging from the gravplates in the ceiling like the victim of a giant bug or something.

Probably Del's way of keeping things a little crazy.

"Whachagot?" Javier asked.

Del brought up a map on his screen.

"Just detected multiple ships emerging from jump in the vicinity," the pilot said, pointing to four red stars on a screen. "Thoughts?"

Probably about two light hours out, so they may have already jumped closer and just not shown up on a sensor. It wasn't like the shuttle was pinging the neighborhood all that hard.

Sneaky went both ways. Right now, it mostly meant *blind*.

"If he follows his usual procedure, that's the transport, two little gunboats as escorts, and Slavkov's personal yacht," Javier observed, as if Del hadn't already been through this briefing more than once. He probably just wanted someone to talk to. "The yacht will drop a shuttle for him and his party, and they'll go somewhere else for a while. The freighter will send down the big lander for the Leviathan. The gun-bunnies are to keep pirates honest, since the freighter has two escorts about as well armed as destroyers for offensive firepower."

"And the lot of you are going to go capture the transport freighter?" Del asked. "Just like that?"

"Fear is a wonderful tool, Del," Javier smiled. "Valko Slavkov is a big fish. Anyone crossing him is likely to have ninjas sent after them. Ergo, nobody would ever dare do what we're about to."

"So, he's bluffing?" Del continued.

Javier felt the shark smile take over his face.

"Don't care," Javier said. "I'm not."

Even gruff, old Del kinda blinked at that. Probably forgot that he was dealing with Navarre today, even if Navarre was just a façade Javier put up when he had to be an asshole.

Slavkov absolutely had it coming.

"Okay, then," Del concluded. "Ready for this?"

"Absolutely," Javier smiled. "How close can you get us?"

"Well, pretty boy there picked a nice flat valley to come to rest in," Del sneered as he flipped the map to an orbital view and zoomed in. "Come night, I can drop you down within about five kilometers on the back side of a ridge. After that, you're on your own. I'll hop back up under cloak and sit out in space watching. Ought to be fun."

"Oh, yeah," Javier agreed. "It'll be a riot."

PART TWO

Afia didn't like hot.

The Yukon Protectorate, where she had grown up, had been a cool place at the best of times. Downright bitter, vicious, nasty freezing in the winter, but only a fool went out in those months. Usually for more beer, if your planning was bad enough to run out.

Desert sand had a way of getting in all the wrong places. Sensitive spots that didn't like scratchy. Made her a touch irritable just contemplating how long it might be before she could get naked and take a good, cool shower again.

But Javier needed her on this mission. And it came with hazard pay. The dragoon was learning to rely on her as well, which was about as high a compliment as you could get from that woman.

Still, front-side-down on the lip of a sandy ridge in the dead of night, looking through binoculars, was not her idea of a good time. Unless there was a cute guy at the other end, with a window just waiting for her to tap on it.

Or something like that.

Heaven forbid she ever sneak out at night and engage in amorous hoolliganisms with strange boys. No, sir. Pure as the driven snow.

Or something like that.

It had at least finally cooled down to being almost tolerable around here, so she wasn't going to bitch too loudly at what she had to deal with.

Sand. Well, mostly rock around here. For a desert, it was more of an ugly scrub of big, exposed stone held together by scraggly bushes. Giant, salmon-and-tan dominos stacked up and covered with dust.

The stone undulated in awkward ways, too, like you had dropped a handful of rocks in the same bathtub at the same time, and then managed to freeze the waves as they crisscrossed each other.

Del had snuck in and put them down not all that far from the Land Leviathan's destination. Hung around just long enough for them to unass all the gear and get it covered, then ambled off like a cat trying to look innocent while they climbed to the top of the low ridge in the darkness and peeked.

She didn't like all the extra weight from the climbing gear they made her wear, and the camo robe with the hood just made her overheat, but that was the cost of doing business today.

Afia found herself at the left end of a line of people, watching the distant bad guys through a line of grass and bushes on the top of one of those ridgelines. All of the main players were well-hidden, with only the combat team not up here.

Afia could see Iqbal Kader out of the corner of her eye, silently and effectively covering her left flank, and she knew the other five men, the ones Javier always referred to with the collective insult *gun-bunnies*, were around behind them against any risk of an ambush.

Knowing this group, there was at least one surface-to-air missile handy. Maybe two. The dragoon didn't do military crap by half-measures. Nor did her team.

So Afia knew she was safe here.

At least as safe as one could be on a hostile, arid plain, getting ready to pull the caper raid of the century on a man that had already tried to kill them at least once.

Afia hadn't truly understood Javier until she saw the cold

fury in that man's eyes after *Svalbard*. She had known angry men. Dated a few over the years. Javier Aritza had a rage that would make bards salivate. Up there with Agamemnon. Or maybe Achilles.

Sing for me, oh muse, a song of righteous destruction visited on well-deserving assholes.

Not that this Slavkov fellow didn't have it coming. Oh, no. His mistake was not killing them on the first try, because Afia didn't like it any more than Javier did, even if she had gotten to be there when a new goddess was born, and make a totally cool new friend out of it.

Two, if you wanted to count Djamila, who was acting almost human these days.

So some good had come of it, even if Afia had to be rolling around in grit, just waiting for it to infiltrate her clothing and gear to get into the places where it didn't belong.

She was going to hate this planet, in another day or so. No ifs, ands, or buts to it.

And out there, the ugliest diamondback rattlesnake in history slithered slowly across the sand towards them on giant treads.

The optics she had were passive, but still packed a pretty good processor suite.

The Land Leviathan was much warmer than the sand and rock around it after dark, so the computer in her binoculars could do a good job of locking on and stabilizing the image, even at a distance of ten kilometers.

It helped that the driver over there had wanted a nice, flat, parking lot for the beast. A few dry creek beds here and there. Couple of stands of things she might call mesquite trees. Nothing to get in the way of the taxi coming to take the beast home.

Kinda reminded her of a family trip through West Texas when she was twelve. Not as hot as Texas, or as ugly. Afia wasn't sure there were places as ugly as Texas.

Still a nasty place.

"Heads up," a call came through the earpiece she had

forgotten about. "Two vessels deorbiting from the east. Now visible. Everyone cover up and close your eyes."

Afia reached up and pulled the hood of her long robe over her head and far enough to cover the binoculars. She tucked her elbows in and rolled just enough onto her right side to pull her feet up, reaching down to make sure the cloth covered everything.

The cloth insulated against thermal signature, as long as you didn't move, and shielded most electronics and metal signatures. It had already morphed into the mixed color of the stone underneath her. If there was no movement to draw the eye, nobody would have a reason to send a sensor pulse this way.

Just another handful of rocks on the ridge. Nothing to see here. Move along.

The noise came along soon enough. Dull roar on her left.

Afia snuck just enough of a peek to spot the two stars descending, and then closed her eyes and turned her face back down to the ground. Both vessels were showing off, flying in tandem formation and landing slowly, almost sedately, on thrusters, rather than swooping in to settle to the ground.

Or maybe she'd been flying with Del too much. You never knew what civilized people were like, after enough time as a pirate.

As soon as the ships dropped into the low bowl in front of them, before they had even touched down, Javier tapped her on the hip and Afia was on her feet.

If everything went right, everyone over there would be focused on landing the executive shuttle for that asshole Slavkov and his guests coming down right next to the Land Leviathan so nobody had to walk any great distance, and didn't have to do it in the oppressive heat of day. So far, all the gossip and sneaky intel that someone had gathered had been on cue.

She didn't want to take the time to look, but knew that most of the Leviathan's crew, and all the support staff for guests, would depart with the big shuttle and follow Slavkov to his next destination, leaving only a skeleton team to drive the Leviathan onto the big lifter and ride it to orbit.

If she really cared, Afia could have looked up and probably spotted the moving stars that were the gunships escorting this bitch between stars.

Sascha and Hajna had already taken off, almost loping down the hill, trusting that there was enough distraction and cover right now, and shortly there would be way too much dust in the air for anyone to spot them.

Everyone else was behind in a compact string. Four of the gun-bunnies were on point, centered on Djamila, while Iqbal and Tom brought up the rear. In between, Afia was making good time next to Farouz. Even Javier was keeping up as they jogged.

She'd seen him working out more, so she knew the science officer could handle a quick four kilometer jog into the thick fog the twin landers had kicked up in the otherwise calm air.

Right on cue, visibility dropped to meters.

Afia could still see Farouz beside her, along with Moore and Spider trailing close behind, and maybe that gun-bunny in front of her was Demyan. Hard to tell when looking at butts moving in dust. Only Galal stood out, and that was only because he was most of a head shorter than the other five.

At least nobody was shooting at them, which was all Afia really cared about.

A small commotion in front of her caused Afia to slow down.

Djamila was standing over one of her guys. Another was kneeling and examining him.

Afia looked, and then managed to hold her stomach down when she saw the guy's leg. His shin wasn't supposed to bend like that. From the growling through gritted teeth, the dude on the ground agreed.

Afia recognized Heydar from the tone.

"Status?" Djamila asked, almost dispassionately.

Afia felt the clock ticking faster in her head. Pretty soon, someone was going to look this way, or maybe just take off. This was no time to stall.

"Clean break," the kneeling medic said. Helmfried. "I can

splint it, but there's no way he can walk any distance on it for a few weeks. Surgery will be required at some point, as well."

"I've got cover and food," Heydar said hoarsely. "Finish the mission and send help when you can."

"There's no space for a medevac," Djamila warned him. "Might be two days. Might be two months."

"What is the problem?" Farouz was suddenly at Afia's side.

Spooky, like he was a ninja or something, except that one was on the other side of the man. Rence Moore.

"Broken leg," Djamila said. "Bringing him slows us too far off the schedule. Leaving him rubs me the wrong way."

"Agreed," Farouz agreed. "I will carry him."

"I outweigh you by twenty-five kilos, old man," Heydar growled angrily.

"So I will not be able to out-shoot everyone else on this team while transporting you," Farouz observed in a tone that made Afia go all cold.

Farouz wasn't kidding. Like maybe he thought he could take anybody here except maybe the dragoon. And the ninja.

Djamila watched for a moment, then nodded.

"Air splint and enough local that he's good to transport," she ordered. "Not so much he's out. Rotate responsibility to put him guarding prisoners and doors when we arrive."

"Roger that," Helmfried said, flipping open his backpack and drawing supplies.

Afia watched the medic wrap a brace around the lower half of Heydar's leg, inflate it, and hit the groaning warrior with a hypospray in less than thirty seconds.

And then Farouz, barely any taller than her, picked the guy up in a fireman's carry in one go and slung the gun-bunny over his shoulder easy, like a bag of rice.

"Move," Djamila ordered, knocking everyone back into motion.

Elapsed time, less than one minute.

Damn, these people really were that crazy, weren't they?

Up ahead, the dust was thinning as they closed. Big bomb

of sand and grit had pushed outwards, and now slowly settling. The transport was huge.

Afia had known the scale they were working with, but it was one thing to hear, and another to actually get close to a ship that was nearly as long as *Hammerfield*, resting on a dozen scorpion legs on the ground in front of her.

Seriously, it was a kilometer long, and at least two hundred meters wide at the nose, shaped like a broadsword lying on its side.

Still, nobody shooting. So far, so good.

If they had been spotted, someone would have done something stupid. Flares screaming into the sky. Pop-up turrets suddenly spitting death. Flying assault marines with chain-swords.

Something.

She was close enough now to actually touch the thing.

From a distance, those legs had looked spindly. Up close, they were dull-gray, redwood trees, ten meters thick at the ankle and widening as they telescoped up into the monster's belly.

Afia joined everyone else as they squatted or kneeled in the shadow of the ship, hiding again under the cloaks that masked them from casual perception.

She knew there were lots of guns, pointed outward in every direction, but all she could see were lumps of sand and outcrops of rock, all innocent and stuff.

Thirty seconds of silence passed.

In the distance, the little yacht was just now cracking open and lowering a landing ramp at the rear. If she hadn't been hiding under the biggest lander she had ever seen, Afia would have thought the other vessel was huge.

Certainly impressive over there, all lit up and painted in gold and chrome. Multi-deck party barge, like when she was a kid, upscaled by several orders of money to a starship just as functional and *way* more tacky.

Flitter limos were emerging from the aft of the Leviathan now. Important people did not walk across sand that might damage expensive shoes. And heaven forbid someone spill a drink crossing rough terrain.

Only the crew walked, moving with rapid deliberation to make it aboard the shuttle in time to be of whatever flunky service these yahoos demanded next.

Soon, the Leviathan would be a ghost town, populated by the leftover engineers who kept the beast fed and mobile. Kinda like the lander looming above her was supposed to be.

The sound of the landing ramp coming down at the aft of the big, metal lander was like an earthquake.

One hundred meters wide. One hundred deep. Sliding on hydraulic hinges that made it move like warm molasses on a cool day. And a deep, profound rumble.

All the lights over there largely vanished as the ramp dropped and obscured everything.

And still, no shooting.

"Spider," Djamila barked quietly, staying off the radio at this phase for absolute secrecy. "Phase two."

Afia had stayed close enough to the lanky, blond Anglo to watch him unfurl from under his cloak like a morning flower.

He kept the poncho on, but flipped it back out of his way, like a true cloak, as he took two long strides and reached up with those huge hands to grab a strut or something.

Serious. Spider. Dude went right up the lander's leg like an insect.

Suddenly, he was ten meters in the air and crossing hand over hand like a kid at a playground.

Afia just shook her head in disbelief. Yoga was fine. Running acceptable. That level of exercise might be a bridge too far. Except how skinny the guy was. There might be something to it, after all, if it kept you skinny. Gotta look that up.

There was a box-thing emerging from the underside of the hull, maybe four meters on a side. Spider crossed to it, settled, and did something magic with his hands.

"Afia," Djamila said. "Phase three."

Afia took a deep breath and stood up, adjusting everything

so it didn't rub wrong. Into all her gear, they had added a harness.

Big, ugly, cold, steel ring just above her belly button. She hadn't liked it. Didn't like it. Wasn't here to bitch.

It wasn't that she had a thing about heights. She had climbed trees as a kid. Every kid did that. This was something else.

Spider was done overhead.

Afia walked close and looked up.

The man had attached a small box to the hull of the transport, and HOPEFULLY SECURED THE DAMNED THING.

A flick of one of those bean-long fingers and a grapple began to descend towards her on a long cable.

Old school.

Javier had gone so starkly primitive as to go beyond stealth, these days. Sure, they could have brought some repulsor platforms and made this easy. Maybe a flight backpack. And that would have shown up on a sensor, somewhere. That level of power expenditure, on those frequencies, would be detected, if nothing else. Just like they stayed off the comm.

Instead they wound up seventy-five meters of high-grade steel cable on a winch and hung it from the underside of the ship. You just needed a cat burglar to place it.

And an engineer crazy enough to ride.

Fortunately, Javier happened to know one.

Click.

She was now bound in unholy matrimony with a landing freighter, symbolized by a giant, cold-steel ring hanging beneath her boobs.

Afia took a deep breath and leaned backwards, relaxing into the cable.

Spider nodded at her. She nodded back. He flipped a switch.

She was flying.

Tinkerbell in a low-budget stage production version of the

Neverland Saga. Complete with the profanities, mostly under her breath.

When she got close, Spider smiled at her. Probably meant to be reassuring. Sure. Afia looked down anyway. No false sense of security about this, thank you.

Spider reached out a hand and slowly turned her to face the big, steel box that was her target.

Ground elevator.

Currently retracted, and it would stay that way. Safety measure. And security.

Anybody could push the big, bronze button to deploy it to the ground automatically.

And set off every damned alarm on the ship overhead.

That was why you needed an engineer.

Afia took a deep breath and pulled a powerdriver out of her thigh pouch with her right hand. Number four bit would be close enough.

She fixed everything in her mind and reached out. Four countersunk machine bolts held the face plate.

The first two came out easy enough.

Number three fell through her fingers. She tried to grab it. Afia stabbed at it with one hand and nearly turned turtle, forgetting where she was.

Hopefully, she'd be able to puke far enough away that it wouldn't land on anyone, if she did that again. This playground wasn't that fun.

She did look down, just in time to see Javier catch the bolt in one hand. Yeah, he probably had been expecting that. Speed was more important than style, right now.

Fourth bolt out. Three in pocket. Faceplate handed off to Spider. Naked machine innards displayed to the world like some sort of electronic burlesque show.

Engineering pornography.

It took all kinds.

Yup. Push THAT button and everything deploys. Including the alarms.

Afia began tracing leads. They hopefully had time to do this right. It would take hours for the snake to eat that deer. The limo hadn't even lifted off yet.

She dropped the powerdriver into its holder and pulled a steel wedge chisel.

Handy, for breaking and entering. Make sure this circuit retains power when you cut that one. Find the signal that tells the system what's happening and lobotomize it by severing a gold thread on an exposed circuit board.

There.

Find the backup, because the bastard who designed the system thought he was being sneaky.

Yup. Snip.

Check for a third one, because I would have.

Bastard. He did, too, didn't he?

Fine.

Trace. Okay, fully isolated?

Yes.

Paranoid mook.

Afia nodded to Spider.

"All good," she said.

Spider let enough line out that he could pull her out of the way, himself hanging from a hook off to one side.

She felt like his latest victim. Or conquest. The man had chewed on a breath mint recently. Cinnamon and wintergreen. Afia wondered what a kiss might taste like. Not the time to find out, but she made a note to circle back later.

That long arm reached out and pressed the bronze button. Silently, the elevator began to go down. Hopefully, nobody aboard the ship would be the wiser.

Or they were all dead.

PART THREE

Javier had his qualms.

Technically, he shouldn't be here on the ground. Sykora and her team could handle the dangerous tasks. Afia was actually doing the job he would have, being all sciencey and an engineer. His place was probably clear out on the edge of the solar system with Suvi and Zakhar Sokolov.

Waiting.

Yeah, screw that.

He was a patient man, or he'd have never made it as a survey scout, or a science officer. But there were limits to his patience.

He watched the descending lift shaft touch the ground and open.

Sykora was the first one in, because of course she was. Javier followed two steps behind her, with more of the first team behind him.

When he thought about it, Javier decided it was rather silly that most of this initial group was female. If Farouz hadn't come along, all of them would have been: Sykora, Hajna, Sascha, and the black widow, Rence Moore. He liked women.

And he did have one advantage over the rest of them. The reason he was here, instead of there.

Rather than pull a gun, like everyone else, Javier reached

into a pouch and pulled out the smaller survey probe. The one that had been Suvi's home for the first year, before he built her the armed one. She couldn't be here, but the sight of it still brought her to mind. Even if they all died on this mission, she would survive. He had beat the pirates.

The first batch, anyway. Sokolov and the nicer ones.

The rest were about to get theirs.

He popped in the power button, checked the configuration, and softballed it into the air as the door to the elevator closed, separating all of them from the outside world. His sidekick had done a serious upgrade on the software, just exactly for this mission.

Pretty walls in the tiny room. Egg-cream color with highlights that were probably real gold, knowing the jackass who had paid for it. Textured floor so nobody slipped.

Djamila looked over at the hovering probe, eyes slightly askance. So did the two pathfinders, but for different reasons. Sascha grimaced quickly, but got over it.

Javier pulled out the board and checked things.

It was going to be like the old days, when the thing was just a flying sensor pack and he had to do all the work. For the last few years, all he had done was push buttons that made it play music for Suvi, or cause rabbits and other cute critters to race across her desk while she flew.

Now it was back to him again.

"How good is it now?" Djamila asked, having been there most of the times it had been used.

"Suvi did a good job automating a number of tasks for me," Javier replied. "Without her in there, I didn't want to worry about shooting, but this one will do wonders. It won't be there to save your ass in a wrestling match, though."

Djamila nodded, holding a pistol in each hand and looking like a northern European Goddess of War.

The Morrigan, come for your soul, as it were.

The lift rose silently, smoothed no doubt by the risk that a pissant like Slavkov might have to use it at some point and it must thus be as even as winter ice.

Javier concentrated on setting the autopilot to hover just high enough that Sykora would clear it if she moved suddenly. Not an easy task with a woman that tall and ceilings this low.

The elevator door opened.

No crew member had been unlucky enough to be close enough to the door to get shot for his curiosity. At least Djamila had a stun pistol in one hand. As did the rest of them.

Sascha stuck a camera probe out just far enough to look both ways, and then nodded at Javier.

All clear.

The probe floated out next, a big, gray pearl hanging perfectly in space as it rotated.

Javier pushed a virtual button labeled *Annoy Carnivorous Bats* and watched the readout come back with an amazing level of detail as the machine went to work. Another of Suvi's inside jokes.

Before Sykora could ask, Javier put the display in three dimensions.

Djamila would be able to absorb the information, probably even hanging upside down and half-drunk. Farouz as well.

They both needed better hobbies.

From here, everything would be hit or miss.

Luck would play a major role as well, since nobody had any idea how this ship was laid out, once you got beyond the design basics of naval architecture.

In the hall, they moved to what cover you could get from slightly-recessed doors, but didn't do anything else. Javier's job was electronic scouting. Afia would disable all the security systems. That required some dedicated tools, and Javier didn't feel like winging it.

He would only get one chance at Valko Slavkov.

Thirty seconds later, the rest of the team joined them.

Javier had spent the time studying the psychological elements of the ship's construction. The walls and hallway here were that same egg-cream. Not white, not yellow. Less gold decoration on the walls. The floors were textured metal in diagonal X shapes, done in a gray that would probably hide any spill or stain. Wide and tall hallways. Maybe four meters across and three and a half tall, with light bars running down the center of the ceiling and both edges, making it almost a perfect movie set in here.

Again, the importance of looking good, on the off-chance that the main guy had to come this way. Javier figured the man'd be pissed if he had to, because that would mean something had gone wrong with the shuttle the rich bastard used.

People would probably end up getting fired and blackballed if he didn't just have them shot. In a lot of these places there was no law but the man with the gun. Even if Slavkov was a legitimate businessman somewhere.

In the end, we're all pirates. I'm just better dressed.

Afia moved close and knelt to study the panel closest to Javier. There weren't any alcoves to duck into, since the hatches were only set back from the hall by about ten centimeters, so the team was strung out on both sides, watching either direction. Somewhere, there would be cross hallways and stairs, plus a few more elevators. Hopefully, this was an engineering level that nobody needed to access while they loaded the Leviathan.

With any luck, Javier had an hour or more before the beast could be driven aboard and secured. That would be enough time, he hoped.

Powerdriver in hand, Afia had the panel off and her nose stuck in, tracing leads and logic.

There was no *Sentience* on this ship or someone would have already noticed them boarding. Javier worked on the presumption that he only had to worry about the bridge crew, since everyone else would be outside for now, or in the cavernous loading bay.

"Seriously?" Afia muttered under her breath.

"What?" Javier fired back, feeling the surge of cold adrenaline fill his belly.

This would not be a pleasant place to die. At least having Djamila and her killers along would make the other guy pay a very high price for his soul.

"Lazy designer," Afia replied with an unpleasant tone. "Everything is hard-wired, instead of controlled from a central system. The dragoon might have been able to hack this system."

"Translate, please?" Javier said.

He liked the girl, but she occasionally wandered down rabbit holes. Still, she was a better engineer than he was at some of the hands-on stuff. Especially security systems.

Javier never asked where she had gotten those particular skills. None of his business.

"With a central system, you control all the functions with passwords and access levels," she explained. "Like we do. This doesn't have anything. Get me to a proper workstation with a keyboard, and I can tell you anything the captain of this tub can. Downside, I can't lock him out, either."

"Internal security cameras?" Djamila asked quietly from her spot at one end of the line.

"Nothing," Afia said. "Looks like sensors on doors opening, but that's tied to life support, in case you have a leak and need to seal frame sections in a hurry. Dumb-ass design."

"Not if everyone's too scared to pull a stunt like this," Javier said. "What is there to steal, after all? And where would you take it?"

"You are going to tell us at some point, right?" Afia turned and batted her eyelashes at him to be a flirt.

A really cute one, too.

"You wouldn't believe me," Javier said. "Sokolov barely did."

She rolled her eyes at that, but quickly began to reassemble the system and screw the faceplate back on. If this worked, someone would have to fix everything they broke. Might as well not leave loose ends around.

"Direction?" Djamila asked him.

"Everyone should be either aft, or headed that way," he replied. "Let's get to the bridge as quietly as possible. Stun anything that moves."

Djamila nodded and whispered a quick set of orders that got her folks moving.

Javier found himself moving in the middle again, flying the

probe, with Spider and Farouz, still carrying the guy with the broken leg like a bag of coffee. Mind-boggling, but the guy was tough enough to impress Djamila, and Javier had seen him move in combat, once upon a time, so he had no doubts just how dangerous Farouz could be when he chose.

Sascha, Hajna, and Moore went first, with Djamila and Afia close behind, maybe five meters away. The other five gun-bunnies brought up the rear after another gap, playing a game of backwards-facing hopscotch as they covered the ass end of the column against surprises. For a group this big, they moved with amazing quiet.

First seal reached.

Unlike the side hatches they had passed, this one was serious. Able to retain a seal across a frame section if the ship suffered damage. Also useful against anything the team carried except missiles. Hopefully, nothing so drastic would be needed.

Afia went to work. Djamila watched over her shoulder.

Javier found a long stretch of wall and put his butt up against it as he focused on tweaking sensor settings. He programmed the system to wash out the sound of the team walking. Hopefully, the Leviathan would make a lot of ruckus when it boarded, so they would feel it in their feet.

Nothing that big could move quietly. Especially not climbing up a shallow ramp into its bolthole.

The rest of the team were all covering their directions of fire. Even Farouz had turned sideways. That let the guy on his back see aft, pistol in one hand against utter catastrophes.

Everyone had a different safety blanket to keep the bogeyman at bay. Javier was flying his.

Javier looked up in surprise as the hatch directly across from him opened.

"Acknowledged," the man in the doorway yelled over his shoulder as he came through, stumbling to a halt as he turned and saw the people around him in what was supposed to be an empty corridor.

For the longest instant, a frozen tableaux as the hatch slid shut behind him.

Shock. Amazement.

Javier was already keyed up and just about to the point of reacting when Farouz took a sudden half step and lashed out with his left hand, a circular swing like a length of chain crashing into the side of the stranger's head with an ugly crunch.

Must have been the right choice. Dude went down like a sack of potatoes.

The gun-bunny on Farouz's back never moved.

Elapsed time, maybe half a second.

"Afia," Javier barked. "Lock this door."

She scampered.

The other side of that hatch was the very front end of the big bay. Hopefully, nobody had been looking at the right moment to see folks like Javier in the hallway when the hatch had opened. If they had, things were about to get ugly.

Javier looked down at the guy.

No blood. Head still on straight. Hopefully, just out cold.

It did give him an idea as Afia quickly popped the panel open and went to work.

"Locked or dead?" she asked, turning to look up at him.

"Seal it," he decided. "If they're coming, make them come a different way. We'll fix it later."

"On it," she replied.

Djamila was inspecting the body on the floor, kneeling with one hand on his neck feeling for a pulse. She had even holstered a pistol for long enough to do that.

"Still alive," she announced, turning to Farouz. "What was that?"

"Crane form," he replied, shrugging in spite of the weight on his shoulder. "Mastoid process strike. Stuns instantly. Rarely kills. Disables a target effectively."

"Yes," she agreed.

Javier could see the pride and warmth in her smile as she looked up at the man.

Ew.

Javier inspected the guy on the floor.

Yeah, just about his size, which meant more or less average.

Maybe too much gut and too little shoulders, but close enough for improv work.

And everyone else in the group was the wrong size, Farouz and one of the bunnies being half a head shorter, with Spider and the rest half a head taller.

"Gimme his uniform," Javier said. "Trojan horse time."

Djamila looked up at him for a moment, then nodded.

Wonder of wonders, she holstered the other pistol and began unbuttoning things.

The victim was in what was obviously a uniform designed by a nimrod that had never actually served, but wanted to pretend he was important. Stupid looking saucer hat with a logo on the forehead. Light blue shirt with lots of buttons and braid. Boards on the shoulders with cute designs embroidered. Long sleeves with French cuffs.

French cuffs? Seriously?

Navy blue slacks with a gold stripe down the seam. Polished black leather shoes.

We'll do without the shoes. Mine are better, anyway.

Javier set the controls for the remote down and dropped his desert cloak. Underneath, a skin-tight, insulated shirt with a light shell jacket over that. The jacket went first.

He dropped on his butt and the boots went next. Pants as well. The deck was cold, but at least he wasn't commando on this run.

Djamila tossed him the man's pants and Javier wriggled into them.

Yup, gonna need a belt. Or a knife to add a notch.

The top was a bad fit, but good enough. Javier left the top two buttons undone, or he might choke himself when he moved.

At least the hat fit.

"Right," he said, standing as he sealed up his boots again. "I'm on point. We'll move quickly and my job is to distract anyone long enough for you to shoot them. Questions?"

There were none. He handed Spider the probe's control

board. It was easy enough to fly, and with a uniform, Javier planned to move much faster than before.

Guile instead of stealth, as it were.

Javier put a hand in a pocket and discovered a hard plastic badge.

Ho ho. Access key. We're going to get into all sorts of trouble, now.

He smiled at the rest of them with a lunatic grin as he pulled it out.

This has just turned into a con job.

Scarily, Djamila grinned back. Like she knew what was coming. She might. She had been there enough times with him.

PART FOUR

DJAMILA PULLED two sets of plastic restraints from a pouch and secured the man on the floor at wrist and ankle. He wasn't important enough to bring along, and Aritza would be moving quickly now. He had that gleam in his eyes. A man about to start surfing an avalanche of fresh manure and come out smelling like a rose. As he always did.

She considered being jealous of the ability, but settled for using the man's luck as a shield.

Djamila rose from the floor and drew both pistols. She had always been ambidextrous, but just enough right-handed that the stunner was there, where it would be the first shot fired instinctively. The beam-cutter could wait for armor and bulkheads.

She nodded curtly at him. Ready to go.

Javier's face got a bit of an angry snarl to it, probably close enough to her own, and he walked to the bulkhead hatch, waving the badge at the sensor as the rest of the team settled into columns.

Guile and audacity. Aritza's signature moves. It was going to be *Shangdu*, all over again.

Djamila glanced both directions just enough to pick up the pathfinders in her peripheral vision and strode forward. The corridor was wide enough to walk three abreast, but they were staying several meters back now.

Aritza on point was a bulwark of armor and misdirection Djamila would use to get close enough to shoot. At this point, anything that moved was a legitimate target, thus the stunner in her right hand, just like most of the rest of her team.

Most.

Galal would have a shaped-charge handy to breach any barrier.

Based on her own dead reckoning, they were almost to the bow now. Over Javier's shoulder, she could see an oversized hatch to port, along the outer edge of the ship, as well as a curve where the corridor rounded towards the exact bow.

Javier stopped at the enormous hatch, glancing only briefly to his right as the path continued that way.

He nodded to himself before turning back to her.

"Up here," he said. "I want to put us right under the bridge facility, as here should be a big service area where he can host parties."

She nodded back.

Nothing more to say.

He badged the door open and she followed two steps behind into a room with a winding ramp that was ten meters across and corkscrewed up so slowly that Djamila could have attached wheels to her boots and worked up a tremendous head of speed to clear the door and blast down the main hallway at a dead sprint.

She considered making it a competitive event by adding armed targets, the final one being the shot that would open the door before you slammed into it.

She smiled and began to ascend, letting Aritza have a full half-turn before following.

Djamila signaled the girls to move the team to the outer edge of the ramp, back from being visible from above, but she stayed close enough to fire upwards a considerable distance if Aritza got into trouble.

Lord knew he was barely competent with a pistol. Suvi had confirmed that she had done all the trick shooting.

The decks on this ship were outsized, matching the personality of a man who would build a Land Leviathan. What starship needed six-meter ceilings?

One intended to show off wealth and power.

Javier surprised her by continuing on past the first level as the ramp continued. But then she considered that the land beast itself was at least thirty meters tall. Having space to work might require a bay six or eight of these decks tall, although she expected that the crew quarters would be a dismal warren of rabbit holes with barely two-meter ceilings.

What good was power and wealth if you didn't get to oppress someone with it? Everything she had heard or experienced about Slavkov and his operation suggested punks, rather than professionals. *Svalbard* had been a telling sign.

Again the winding. Javier passed the third floor at a brisk march, trusting in her by only glancing back on rare occasion to make eye contact across the half circle.

His eyes still had a killing gleam in them.

Djamila wasn't above letting the man get himself killed here. But that was no longer a necessity.

Many things had changed since the goddess had taken possession of *Excalibur*. The Lady of the Lake. With the help of her friends, maybe even Djamila Sykora could change. And trade up for the problem of two capable men who both wanted her, the woman who had always been the ugliest duckling in any pond.

Fourth deck. Aritza again paused to look back at the caravan behind him, but continued. Fernandez had finally gotten the hang of flying the probe well enough to send it up the column of empty space in the middle of the spiral, tracking even with her but providing a solid scanning arc against hidden surprises.

Fifth deck. Javier apparently had what he wanted. She caught up to him on a half spiral and waited.

"The bow is about two hundred meters across," he said out of the blue.

She nodded, familiar with the general layout Suvi had been able to scan without focusing a beam on the ship.

"Based on the rest of the architecture, I'm guessing that this is the level I want, even though this thing goes up more," he continued. "If you settle on treads when you park, the back of a room on this level ought to be looking right across the top of the Leviathan."

"Would he want a higher view?" Djamila asked.

"Probably," Javier nodded up at her as the team began to catch up. "But I bet we'd set off alarms if we suddenly went into officer country, being only peons. Now, we need to get sneaky."

Djamila turned in place to survey the group. She had assembled a team of experts across a variety of fields, knowing Javier's general plans and style, but having no greater idea than he did about the facts on the ground.

"Moore, team one, with me," she said. "Afia and Farouz with the pathfinders as team two. The rest of you are team three. Heydar will remain here and secure our rear."

The tiny woman killer nodded the barest amount. Djamila was aware that Rence Moore hadn't shown off her talents and training to anyone else on this team, so only she and Farouz had seen the assassin move.

Djamila turned back to Javier.

"Go," she said.

He nodded and squared his shoulders, doing *something* that turned him from a thief into an important crewmember on a mission. Djamila hadn't gotten the hang of that level of acting, but she had learned enough from the man, and from others, like Dr. Wilhelmina Teague, to understand it happening.

Aritza held out a hand to the sensor panel and listened for a chirp as it unlocked. Bolts withdrew and the hatch slid aside. He went through at a crisp march, not looking back.

Djamila followed him into another world. She could trust that Moore would move so silently as to be undetectable.

The floors here were carpeted in a vast sea of green. Not a particularly expensive installation, but a radical change from the metal floors on the rest of the vessel. Wood paneling on the walls turned the room earthy, a tone matched by turning the lights down a single notch on the scale, from harsh to adequate.

Furniture around the walls of the large space suggested a reception area, with both sofas and standing tables. A long counter-top that would be turned into a bar by the arrival of bottles and staff. That door to the right of the bar probably led to a kitchen where caterers could whip up mobile finger food.

Djamila decided that it must be used when the vessel was delivered to a new planet, a party for everyone who had arrived to partake of a new adventure.

Dilettantes and Philistines. It probably devolved into orgies at the slightest provocation. Those were the sort of people that would.

Aritza started to cross the area towards a pair of oversized doors on the far end of the room. As Djamila made to move with him, she realized that the back wall was transparent and overlooked the monstrous landing bay. Lights from the far end had just started to fill the space.

Headlights.

"Hold," she said, just loud enough to get his attention.

He turned back with an unvoiced growl in his eyes. Djamila nodded to the window.

He looked, absorbed, and nodded.

"With me," he said. "The rest sneak as you can."

It was insane. Walk right across an open window just as the Land Leviathan was starting to load?

Yes.

Audacity.

Suspicious people act suspicious. One person with Aritza at this distance would not excite the viewer. A whole mob would.

Rence Moore was already short. And had no weapon in her hands. Djamila watched her double over to hands and feet, like a moving yoga pose whose name she didn't know, and scamper across the floor almost as fast as Djamila and Javier walked it.

Djamila hazarded a quick glance to the side as they passed out of the immediate view from the bay. Nothing seemed wrong. No yells. No alarms. No shots impacting the shield.

Good enough. Behind her, the rest of the team dropped and began to crawl below the level of the windows. Afia would hack the door and bring the team through behind them.

They would have to catch up as they could. For now, the three of them would have to handle everything.

Djamila was wearing her normal field uniform of long, heavy pants tucked into field boots. Long button-up tunic over a t-shirt. Everything in a dark-gray/red spackle pattern that distracted the eye inside a ship painted gray. Rence Moore wore something similar, but baggier and looser, hiding the woman inside and providing space for her to secrete weapons and gear.

The next door awaited, closed and resolute, but for the little light on one side of the frame.

Javier waved his badge at the scanner panel and it slid aside. More carpet, more paneling. A long, narrow hallway that seemed to run forever. They passed through and began to penetrate deeper into the whale's belly.

A man turned a corner ahead and looked up from what he was reading on a tablet.

"Who are you?" he asked/yelled.

Fifty-five meters. Right at the effective edge of a stun pistol.

Djamila shot him twice for good measure.

They broke into a jog. Shots fired might set off internal alarms in this section. Others might come along.

The target was down. She could have skipped the second shot, fired as fast as the pistol's batteries would cycle, but training was training. He had already succumbed to the first.

This man's uniform was more impressive than the first one Javier had stolen. She and Moore kept watch while Javier looted the man's pockets and came up with his security badge, tucking the first one away.

"Upgrade," he chortled as he stood.

Moore was peeking around the corner the man had emerged from. Nobody was coming from the far end of the hallway. Her people were behind them somewhere, covering the rear.

"Him?" she asked.

"Leave him," Javier replied. "He won't be a threat for an hour. It'll be over by then, one way or the other."

Djamila agreed. Phase One would be done. The rest of Aritza's insane plan would start to roll at that point.

"We should be exactly below the bridge now," he said, glancing at the ceiling.

"Stairs and lift here," Moore said, pointing down the hallway aft as she broke her self-imposed reticence.

"Stairs," Djamila and Javier said almost in unison.

Never get trapped on an elevator in a combat situation. No good will come of it.

They turned the corner into a short corridor with a single lift door in the center and hatches on each side that would access the stairs.

"You two split," Javier said.

Djamila considered the options and turned to the flight of stairs on the right.

"You go with him," she ordered.

Rence Moore was as much shorter than Aritza as Djamila was taller. She could hide behind the man when the door opened and probably be missed.

Javier handed Djamila his spare keycard.

"Here," he said, turning and disappearing through the door leading to the other staircase.

Djamila took the steps three at a time. Up seventeen, eyes tracking above her. Platform. Turn. Up seventeen more. Landing. Turn.

She spotted the door at the top of the next set of stairs. It had a glowing spot to one side for a badge. Hopefully, the first prisoner had enough access to make it to the bridge.

Seventeen steps and she was standing before it. She ignored the next flight of stairs going up. Javier would be here when he opened the door.

Djamila holstered her beam-cutter and badged the lock.

It beeped at her, and nothing.

She tried again, just in case.

Failure.

Probably, a security light had just started flashing on somebody's console. Depending on how busy things were, nobody might notice.

As if on cue, the whole vessel rumbled with a very mild earthquake as the Land Leviathan hit its ramp and began to ascend into the encircling embrace of the ugly dachshund hound.

Djamila smiled to herself.

Guile and audacity.

She stuck the badge into her breast pocket, holstered her stunner, and pulled the beam-cutter.

Working quickly, she adjusted the power settings down into a tool rather than a weapon.

Not many people were even aware you could use a beam-cutter this way, having forgotten the origins of the device as a short-range plasma cutter.

It worked so much better as a hand-held particle cannon.

Most of the doors so far had been simply locked. And this one was not a frame airlock. Just a barrier against access, and even that mostly psychological.

Djamila picked out a spot in the center of the frame, closest to the badge reader, and fired a shot into the jamb.

Sparks, but not a lot of noise.

Somewhere, a fire system was probably thinking about waking up. A Damage Control board probably had a light suddenly flashing yellow.

Djamila fired a second shot. The door clicked in some esoteric way that told her she had cut the locking bar. Standard designs were meant to be breached this way in an emergency.

This was close enough to an emergency.

She reset the beam-cutter and then holstered it.

With both hands, she leaned her weight into the door and felt it move sideways. A centimeter of motion and the motors suddenly engaged, pulling it the rest of the way.

Djamila drew her main stunner as well as the backup she always carried in a shoulder rig. Now would be the time to take out an entire room in one go. Pity none of her team would be able to see this Hogan's Alley. Maybe she would play back the internal security footage for them later as training footage, after she had rung up another high score.

Aritza had just opened the other door and stepped out onto the rear of the ship's command deck.

It was mostly empty here. This alcove they were in was under an overhanging balcony or mezzanine, the space above probably being where the party would go so that nobody got in the way of professional officers flying the ship.

And so none of the crew accidentally got their proletariat germs on important people.

Not that Djamila had strong feelings about social status, being the daughter of a lower decks crewman and an exotic dancer.

Javier stepped out first, smiling up at her as he did, like she was the second shark at a frenzy. She might be, all things considered. She didn't see Moore, either emerging with him or in the doorway, so she presumed the woman had gone up another level.

Of the three of them, Rence Moore was the least likely to kill any random stranger she found up on that vastly oversized platform, if for no other reason that she wasn't personally, emotionally, involved.

Djamila Sykora had been around starships and warships for most of her life. Both in service and later as a pirate. She was used to large crews and redundancy.

The size of the transport kept throwing her assumptions off. This vessel existed solely to provide transportation for the Land Leviathan. Nothing else. Nothing *grander*.

It wasn't even a shuttle designed to rendezvous with a larger vessel in orbit. No, it was just a shell. Engines powerful enough to get the vessel into orbit. Jump drives capable of getting it to the next destination with a minimum of fuss, but no great speed. It served no other purpose than catering to a man's ego.

Djamila's face hurt from scowling so hard as she stepped out and went tactical.

Two-level bridge. Well, two plus the balcony above her.

Back to metal floors. Walls no longer wood-lined, but painted a stark white that would probably show every smudge and cobweb. Javier walked out ahead of her, to a bannister that ran athwart the path, psychologically directing people right or left down smooth, circular ramps to the bridge itself, down two meters in a manner like a sunken living room, rather than a separate deck.

Captain's chair, facing forward. Elaborate and over-wrought. Like the man sitting in it now. Or, at least the back of his head, with a bald spot surrounded by a ring of brown and white hair.

Three crew stations in front of that, arranged to complete a diamond, all facing forward. Filled with three crew members present and watching their boards.

Big, transparent porthole at the front of the bridge, three meters tall by roughly nine wide. The blast screens were open now, revealing the night sky and the place on the distant hillside where her team had lain in wait.

Javier walked right up to the bannister, paused, and gestured with his head for her to join him. Three long, silent strides put her at his left, both stunners still in hand.

She glanced back and up. Javier was standing about two meters in front of the edge of the balcony overhead. She couldn't see anyone at the near edge, but that didn't mean it was open.

Hopefully, Moore was up there and covering their backs.

"Captain, I have a security alarm," one of the crewmen said out loud, staring at his board.

"Nobody move, and nobody has to get hurt," Javier ordered the room in a voice big enough for a parade ground.

All four men started at the sound. Three of them turned towards the rear.

Djamila shot the fourth one, seated left center, as his hand moved towards what she assumed was an alarm.

Bad choice. At least both hands were stunners this time.

The other men turned whiter. And froze in place.

Javier went to the right, down and around the ramp.

Djamila crab-walked left, keeping the three prisoners covered as she did.

"Who are you?" the captain demanded.

Fortunately, the man was bright enough to remain perfectly still in his chair as he did so. Djamila might have considered wounding him with the beam-cutter secured in the holster. As an example.

"Captain Navarre," Javier oozed angry malignance over the words. "The pirate."

At least the captain of the transport knew the name. He shuddered once, but got hold of himself quickly.

"What's the meaning of this?" he said, controlling himself.

Djamila couldn't tell if the man was angry or fighting not to wet himself right now. The voice kept going different directions.

"All three of you, out of your chairs, now," Javier ordered. "I will not say it again."

The two crewmen moved like ejection seats had gone off. The captain took a moment longer. The last man was already a puddle on the floor.

Djamila directed them up against the view port and sneered at them from a safe distance.

Javier moved to where he could speak without yelling, but never got between her and the man on the right. He did understand lines of fire, if nothing else.

"This is a hijacking," he said cheerily. "If you behave, I promise to drop you someplace nice and safe when we're done here."

Always the master of the one-liner, she waited the beat for him to drop the bombshell on them.

"I only kill pirates," he continued. "And right now, you haven't convinced me you're pirates. Let's keep it that way?"

The two crew nodded enthusiastically. Like men for whom this was just a job in a galaxy with more people than work. The captain got an angry look. Remained perfectly still, but wanted to gesture angrily, except for the giant woman holding two pistols on him.

"This vessel belongs to Valko Slavkov," the man thundered.

"Do you have any idea what he'll do to you when he catches you?"

"He's already tried to kill me twice," Javier retorted savagely. "If that's the hill you want to die on, be my guest."

That got through the man's bluster. The older captain recoiled and blinked several times. Lizard brain taking over as the higher functions shut down.

"No," the captain replied. "No. Not at all."

"Good," Javier's voice softened. "Now, there is a crew down here that needs to be controlled. I have an entire fireteam of killers just outside this room, but I'd rather not have them massacre your men. And then there are two escorts in orbit that you need to convince all is well when we lift. I have a warship hiding at the edge of the system. A big one. Capable of crushing those two escorts like empty beer cans. But they're just folks doing a job, same as you. Right? With your help, they'll all get to go home to their families tomorrow."

Djamila flashed back in her memory to the two men that had escaped her strike team on *Svalbard*. She had been all set to pursue them into the storage warrens. All fifty-three kilometers of tunnel.

Captain Navarre had convinced them to happily surrender with the same sort of carrot and stick.

Aritza/Navarre was one of the few people Djamila had ever met as utterly ruthless as she was. Zakhar and Farouz were close. Perhaps a handful of others.

And Navarre had returned the men unharmed, matching his promise. That news had apparently gotten around as well. The captain sagged, but it appeared to be mostly in relief.

"Yes," he said. "Your word of honor?"

Honor? From a pirate?

But this was *Navarre*. The killer. The pirate captain who had annihilated Abram Tamaaz. And escaped both traps at *Svalbard*.

And kept his word.

"Absolutely, Captain," Javier replied in a professional tone. "Your ransom and your parole on getting us out of the system safely."

"And Slavkov?"

"He's next on my list, Captain," Javier promised in a voice so utterly drained of emotion that Djamila felt a surge of adrenaline course through her like an icicle.

A sudden sound caused Djamila to leap hard to her left, bouncing up into the air and half-pirouetting as she did. One pistol remained on the three captives. The other sought a target.

Time slowed to a still.

There.

A body collapsing and tumbling bonelessly over the railing from the balcony.

She fired into him twice anyway. Reflex.

Movement above and beyond the falling target. Djamila centered the pistol on it before she processed the image.

Rence Moore.

Other movement. One up, one down.

A pistol falling at the same speed as the man coming off the balcony.

A disk, perhaps four centimeters across by one thick. Black, with two red lights flickering. Arcing into the air as it might do if someone like Rence Moore had thrown it into a man's head hard enough to bounce. With a stun charge grounded on impact. An electric charge heavy enough to knock a horse over.

Djamila smiled, and landed on the deck again, a meter to her left and half turned.

Nobody else had even had time to react.

The man from the balcony struck the floor like an errant sack of potatoes.

Javier glanced at her for confirmation.

Djamila nodded.

The science officer turned to look up at the balcony.

Moore flowed down to the rail with the silent elegance of an approaching glacier.

"I owe you five drachma," the quiet assassin said in a quiet voice.

"I'm just surprised you didn't say some goofy catchphrase to distract the guy first," he replied. "Like they do in the vids."

"Farouz broke me of that habit, early on," Moore commented drily, with just a ghost of a grin.

Djamila felt a surge of pride as she turned back to the three surviving prisoners. Javier just laughed out loud as he joined her.

"What do you even want with the Land Leviathan?" the captain asked, utterly perplexed. "You'll never survive getting a ransom for it."

"I'm not here for a ransom," the science officer said. "I'm after revenge."

"But there's no place in the galaxy you can hide something like that," the older captain retorted, utter confusion writ on his features.

"You don't understand," Javier explained. "But that's okay. I plan on taking the Leviathan to Slavkov and his friends. *Next.*"

Djamila suppressed the shudder that wanted to ripple through her body, both at the words, and the tone.

Javier Aritza/Eutrupio Navarre was a ruthless man. A killer. She could appreciate that in the man, having just spent several years maneuvering to kill him in what any witnesses would have to rate an apparent accident.

What he had planned for the second part of his revenge was a scheme so grand, so audacious, that nobody in the galaxy would be able to anticipate it.

And she was going to help.

READ MORE!

Be sure to pick up the other books in The Science Officer series!

The Science Officer
The Mind Field
The Gilded Cage
The Pleasure Dome
The Doomsday Vault
The Last Flagship
The Hammerfield Gambit
The Hammerfield Payoff

You can also get volumes 1-4 collected together in
The Science Officer Omnibus 1

Volumes 5-8 will be collected in *The Science Officer Omnibus 2*,
available January 2018

ABOUT THE AUTHOR

Blaze Ward writes science fiction in the Alexandria Station universe: The Jessica Keller Chronicles, The Science Officer series, The Doyle Iwakuma Stories, and others. He also writes about The Collective as well as The Fairchild Stories and Modern Gods superhero myths. You can find out more at his website www.blazeward.com, as well as Facebook, Goodreads, and other places.

Blaze's works are available as ebooks, paper, and audio, and can be found at a variety of online vendors (Kobo, Amazon, iBooks, and others). His newsletter comes out quarterly, and you can also follow his blog on his website. He really enjoys interacting with fans, and looks forward to any and all questions-even ones about his books!

Never miss a release!

If you'd like to be notified of new releases, sign up for my newsletter.

I only send out newsletters once a quarter, will never spam you, or use your email for nefarious purposes. You can also unsubscribe at any time.

http://www.blazeward.com/newsletter/

ABOUT KNOTTED ROAD PRESS

Knotted Road Press fiction specializes in dynamic writing set in mysterious, exotic locations.

Knotted Road Press non-fiction publishes autobiographies, business books, cookbooks, and how-to books with unique voices.

Knotted Road Press creates DRM-free ebooks as well as high-quality print books for readers around the world.

With authors in a variety of genres including literary, poetry, mystery, fantasy, and science fiction, Knotted Road Press has something for everyone.

Knotted Road Press
www.KnottedRoadPress.com

www.ingramcontent.com/pod-product-compliance
Lightning Source LLC
Chambersburg PA
CBHW071836190726
48292CB00005B/1797